# J. B. Priestley

## Low Notes
## on a High Level

### A Frolic

GREAT  NORTHERN

First published in Great Britain by
William Heinemann Ltd 1954

This edition published 2020 by:
Great Northern Books
PO Box 1380, Bradford, West Yorkshire, BD5 5FB
www.greatnorthernbooks.co.uk

ISBN: 978-1-912101-44-3


Design by David Burrill


CIP Data
A catalogue for this book is available from the British Library


For more information contact
the J. B. Priestley Society at jbpriestleysociety.com

J. B. Priestley was born in Bradford in 1894. He was educated locally and later worked as a junior clerk in a wool office. After serving in the army throughout the First World War he went to Trinity Hall, Cambridge before setting up in London as a critic and renowned essayist. He won great acclaim and success with his novel *The Good Companions*, 1929. This and his next novel *Angel Pavement*, 1930, earned him an international reputation. Other notable novels include *Bright Day*, *Lost Empires* and *The Image Men*.

In 1932 he began a new career as a dramatist with *Dangerous Corner*, and went on to write many other well-known plays such as *Time and the Conways, Johnson Over Jordan, Laburnum Grove, An Inspector Calls, When We Are Married, Eden End, The Linden Tree* and *A Severed Head* which he wrote with Iris Murdoch. His plays have been translated and performed all over the world and many have been filmed.

In the 1930s Priestley became increasingly concerned about social justice. *English Journey*, published in 1934, was a seminal account of his travels through England. During the Second World War his regular Sunday night radio *Postscripts* attracted audiences of up to 14 million. Priestley shored up confidence and presented a vision of a better world to come.

In 1958 he became a founder member of The Campaign for Nuclear Disarmament and later in life represented the UK at two UNESCO conferences.

Among his other important books are *Literature and Western Man*, a survey of Western literature over the past 500 years, his memoir *Margin Released*, and *Journey Down a Rainbow* which he wrote with his third wife, the archaeologist Jacquetta Hawkes. J. B. Priestley refused both a knighthood and a peerage but accepted the Order of Merit in 1977. He died in 1984. His ashes were buried near Hubberholme Church in the Yorkshire Dales.

# Introduction

*Low Notes on a High Level* was published in 1954, both in the UK and USA. As was his custom, my father gave me a copy, by chance the American edition. Early in 1957, I began my career in films at the bottom of the ladder, and gradually climbed up. In the summer of 1963 I was going for a holiday to Southern Spain, when my father and his then agent found some money and invited me to write a screen version of *Low Notes*. I took my copy plus a notebook and sat by the hotel pool jotting down the scenes. But my experience of films was still very limited, and I was no scriptwriter. My version was uninspired, and thankfully has not survived. On rereading *Low Notes*, there was much I had forgotten, and much to treasure. In our interview for my TV film about him (*Time and the Priestleys*, 1984), he had told me that he had to enjoy what he was writing, very understandable from a man who had spent most of his working life at his typewriter day after day. As a youth growing up in Bradford, he particularly loved the Music Hall and the comics. When he visited Hollywood, he relished spending time with Chaplin and Groucho Marx. We can share his pleasure in inventing his admirable bunch of eccentrics, the curious foreigners with their absurd deep instruments. Pure slapstick of the best. Plus the Schnapps-sunlight, and my father's love of music. So much enjoyment, one can imagine his delight sitting creating in his study aglow with pleasure.

*Tom Priestley is one of Britain's most highly acclaimed film editors. He won a BAFTA in 1967 for his work on the now cult classic* Morgan: A Suitable Case for Treatment *and was Oscar nominated in 1972 for* Deliverance *directed by John Boorman. He has worked on numerous prize-winning films with many talented film-makers including Karel Reisz, Lindsay Anderson, Bryan Forbes, Michael Radford, Jack Clayton, Blake Edwards and Roman Polanski. He now spends his time more in the world, lecturing on film editing and promoting his father's life and work. He is both President of The Bradford Playhouse and The J. B. Priestley Society.*

*Tom Priestley in 1963 in Spain.*

# Low Notes
# on a High Level

## A Frolic

## J. B. Priestley

MY DEAR PETE,

Do you remember—it was two or three years ago, and you were driving me down to Wattisham—how you laughed at my story of the monster bass instruments, and how, later, you expressed much disappointment when I told you I had done nothing with the story? Well, here it is at last, and I am putting your name here to remind you that you are partly responsible for this jaunt. I hope there is in your affection, as I know there is in mine, a special place for the occasional frolics of serious writers— Stevenson's *Wrong Box*, for instance. If there is, perhaps you can manage to squeeze this story into a small corner of that place.

Yours ever,
J. B.

# CONTENTS

Chapter                                                     Page

1.    A MORNING AT RADIO CENTRE                       13

2.    MR. DOBB SAYS NO                                26

3.    THE STORY BREAKS                                44

4.    SCHNAPPS                                        56

5.    NOVELTIES                                       68

6.    DOBB IS HEARD                                   83

7.    THE BEARDED LIFE                                94

8.    RATHER A FULL DAY                               115

9.    LAST LOW NOTES                                  141

# CONTENTS

# CHAPTER I

# A MORNING AT RADIO CENTRE

ON THE fifth floor of Radio Centre, the headquarters of the English Broadcasting Company, a young man called Alan Applerose was sauntering along the main corridor. He was a swarthy and handsome young man, whose melancholy dark face faintly lit with impudence made him immediately attractive to women. (He was, however, unaware of this attraction and inclined to be diffident with them.) By vocation he was a composer of serious music but earned his living as Assistant Musical Director to the E.B.C. At this moment, while drifting along the corridor, he was trying to find a second subject for the slow movement of his *Suite for Strings*. He was so engrossed that he failed to notice the fair girl in the blue coat, and almost knocked her down.

"Oh!" cried the girl, clutching at him.

"Terribly sorry." And he would have passed on but she detained him, keeping one hand on his sleeve and looking up at him with large eyes, sea-green and rather slanting. Had he not been a very modest young man, he might have noticed that these eyes were shining with admiration.

"I was sent up here," said the girl, "to find Miss Mildred Povey. Please can you tell me where she is?"

"I'll take you to her. I'm just going to see her myself. She's in the end studio, rehearsing something for the Fourth Programme. It's something," he added without enthusiasm, "called *No Unicorns on Thursday*."

"Oh—one of those."

"Yes, one of those. A typical Fourth Programme job. Sprung verse, whimsy, and gobbets of Freud. This way."

"What's Miss Povey like?" asked the girl, as they moved off together.

"Mildred? Oh—well—she's tall, handsome, and—er—very

intelligent. As a matter of fact," he added, again without any obvious enthusiasm, "we're supposed to be engaged."

"Oh!" The girl sounded discouraged. "That seems a pity."

Alan waited for her to enlarge on that statement, but when it was clear she had no more to say, he observed, "It's not a good time to catch her when she's rehearsing, but they'll probably be having a break — and anyhow she wants to talk to me about the music — so that's where you nip in. It might help if you told me your name."

"She won't know it, though. It's Inga Dobb."

"Ingadobb?"

"No. Inga — Christian name. Surname — Dobb."

"I get you. My name's Alan Applerose."

"You're lucky. I think that's a delightful name. I wish I was called Inga Applerose."

"Well, I'd just as soon be Alan Dobb. Except that it sounds a bit comrade-ish," he continued thoughtfully. "Tone poems for steel workers — that sort of thing. Here we are." But he did not open the studio door. "Not asking for work, are you, Miss Dobb?"

"Yes." She looked at him hopefully. It was then he first noticed that she was an uncommonly pretty girl. "Reading poetry."

"Why?" He sounded gloomy.

"I've a nice voice — I like poetry, some anyhow — and I want to earn some money."

"Well, we'll try. But let me handle it."

They found inside the studio a fairly large cast of performers. The older types were either yawning or reading newspapers; the younger were looking eager and creative. A pianist and an oboe-player sat there in despair, rather like gangsters who had been kidnapped by a rival mob. Mildred Povey was tall and haughty and sufficiently handsome, but Inga Dobb saw at once that she was idiotically dressed, looking like a school-mistress pretending to be a Toulouse-Lautrec character. She ignored the newcomers and continued her argument with one of the actors, a red-blond untidy youth, a sort of wilted chrysanthemum.

"But, darling," the young actor was protesting, "I feel I *am* integrated here — "

"No, no, Derek," cried Mildred. "Don't you *see*? You know the Seal Woman isn't your mother — you can't feel integrated yet — "

And she led him away from the others, both talking at once.

"How's it going, Alan boy?" This was the pianist, a fat cynical man, probably without a soul. "Are *you* feeling integrated this morning?" He bestowed an enormous wink upon Inga.

"No," said Alan.

"That's because the Seal Woman isn't your mother." He winked again at Inga. "Where do you find these smashing blondes?"

"Don't be low, Charlie. Mildred sent a message to my office, asking me to come up. What's the matter with this score?"

"Everything," said the oboe-player. "You'll have to sit up with it, old man. These amateur pansy jobs get worse and worse. I don't know who this chap is, but nobody's told him yet about the oboe."

"It's a stinker, Alan. For oboe and strings." The pianist came towards them, holding out the score. "That's what he thinks. Wait till the strings try it. I'm just vamping along trying to bring in the *maestro* here. Take a look." He himself took a, very lecherous, look at Inga, who tried to pretend he did not exist. But he was not a sensitive man. "Now, now, now—just because I'm old and fat and need a shave. I—"

"We'll go back to the Pine Forest Chorus," cried Mildred, now taking charge again. Then she saw that the musicians were not at their posts. "Well—really—"

However, at that moment two women arrived with the mid-morning coffee, and Mildred realized that she would have to leave the Pine Forest Chorus until after the break. She saw too that Alan had arrived. "I don't know *what's* the matter with the music," she began as she moved towards them. "Oh—you're looking at it, are you? Well, what's wrong? Edward swore this boy was absolutely brilliant."

"Not at this, he isn't," said the oboe-player.

Mildred ignored him, but in the process of ignoring him she caught sight of the dazzling and hopeful Inga. "Yes? What do you want?"

"Oh—yes," cried Alan, looking up from the score. "Mildred, this is—er—Miss Inga Dobb, who's come to see you about reading poetry."

"Well—really!" It was obvious that Mildred was angry with Alan, angry with Inga, angry with the whole E.B.C. "In the middle of rehearsal! If I've told them once, I've told them fifty times. Allowing people up! I believe they do it specially to annoy me." She gave Inga one hard look. "I can't possibly see you. Please go away."

"Now look, Mildred," Alan rashly protested, "the girl's here. You're having a break—"

"Did you bring her in?"

Before Alan could reply, Inga herself cut in. "I met him outside and asked him where you were—"

"I'm not talking to you." She turned to Alan.

Again, Inga spoke first. "Do you have to be bad-tempered and rude, Miss Povey?"

The coarse pianist laughed coarsely. As the exasperated Mildred swept round to extinguish him, her arm was caught by one of the actresses, a large middle-aged woman who, like many unsuccessful middle-aged actresses, was at once sweetly thoughtful and grimly determined.

"Mildred darling, I want to slow up the Seal Woman—"

"Not now, Margaret, *please*!" Mildred shook herself free.

"But, darling, I simply don't feel her *racing* along like that. Pace, yes. I'm *mad* about pace, as you ought to *know*, darling—"

"I simply won't have her mooing like an old cow," Mildred shouted.

"She's an old seal, dearie," said the pianist, not really being helpful.

"Oh, you shut up. Alan, where are you going?"

"I'm going," he replied with brave deliberation, "down to the canteen—to have some coffee. I'll take this score with me—these chaps say they can't play it anyhow—"

"Dead right, old man," said the oboe-player.

"But if it's as bad as I think it is," Alan continued, still deliberate, still brave, "you'd better give it back to Edward, who can work on it with his brilliant chum."

"They might help to slow up the Seal Woman," the actress suggested. "Tell them, darling."

"And what about getting Derek integrated earlier?" said the pianist. "They could do it with the violas."

"What's this about me?" And Derek was descending upon them.

16

As Mildred exploded, Alan hurriedly left the studio, only to discover that Miss Dobb was running after him. "Wait for me," she cried, "wait for me."

"Why should I wait for you, Miss Dobb?"

"Because," breathless but smiling, "I thought you'd like to give me a cup of coffee in the canteen, Mr. Applerose. I really do adore Applerose. I think I'll marry you." She was now trotting by his side. "First, to get Applerose—"

"There's nothing to prevent you calling yourself Applerose, though I'd rather you didn't—"

"Secondly, to stop you marrying Mildred, which I think would be a great mistake."

"We'll take the lift. Here we are." He regarded her gloomily. "Mildred wasn't at her best this morning. After all, it's no joke producing a thing like *No Unicorns on Thursday*. And she'd hoped to be in Television long before now. Nobody cares much about the poor old Fourth Programme any longer, and Mildred rather likes publicity." The lift arrived. "Basement, please."

"She's not bad-looking," said Inga thoughtfully, "but who told her to wear that kind of outfit? Quite wrong. Are you interested in women's clothes?"

"Not in the least. Never notice what they're wearing. I'm interested in music—dry-fly fishing—and cigars. But of course I can't afford much fishing—or cigars."

"The uncle I live with loves cigars—enormous ones. He smokes them all the time."

"Then he must be very, very rich," said Alan severely.

"No, he isn't. He buys cigars instead of paying income-taxes."

"What a wonderful idea!" He regarded her with a new respect. "I'd like to meet your uncle."

"You'd have to spend a lot of time with me first before you could do that. He doesn't meet people. He says he's had enough of them—and wants to retire from the human race."

"He's got the right idea," said the liftman. "And this is the basement. All change!"

They went along to the canteen, which was still fairly quiet, rather sad, and smelt as if nothing but tomato soup had been served in it for months. Miss Dobb, who was anything but a poker-faced type, stared about her with obvious disgust. "Why has it to be like this?"

"I don't know. I don't run this building—only help with the music. Do you want biscuits with your coffee?"

"Yes, please. In any Scandinavian country a place like this would be clean and bright and gay."

"I'm sure it would. Though I don't know that I want to feel gay down here. And why drag in the Scandinavian countries?"

"Because I half-belong to one of them. Through my mother. Do you *ever* want to feel gay?"

"Not often."

While they were taking the first sips of coffee, which was hot if not strong, she gave him several long sea-green looks, shadowed by regret. "I'm afraid," she announced finally, "that you look more interesting than you really are, Mr. Applerose."

He showed no concern, clearly felt none. "I've been told that before, so there's probably something in it." There now arrived at their table one of the cleaning women, who was going round with a sort of garbage-collector rather like a small warming-pan, and into this she swept from the tables the crusts, bits of buns, cigarette-ends and matches. Muttering malevolently, she opened the lid of this thing almost under their noses. Inga pushed back her chair, and regarded the woman with horror.

"I know," said Alan gloomily, as the woman moved on. "Don't say it. And bear in mind it's much worse when they do it just as you're starting lunch or dinner. Nobody behaves like that even in a dock-side pub. Only in these whacking great organizations. It's the new barbarism."

She waited a moment or two for him to continue. "Go on talking. I like you much better when you begin to talk."

"And I don't like you at all, Miss Dobb, when you hand me that line of patter. Just nibble your biscuits. Hello—here's my boss."

She stared at the bulky figure in the doorway. "Isn't it Sir Lancelot Telly? I thought so. He's looking for you."

"He's seen me," said Alan regretfully.

Sir Lancelot came bounding across. Although large and stout, this famous conductor could bound and bounce. At a first glance he suggested a squire in an old-fashioned musical comedy; he was wearing a bold check coat rather long and full, a bright yellow waistcoat, and baggy tweed trousers; his enormous pink face might have been made-up, and probably was. He reminded Inga somehow of puffed wheat.

"Alan, my boy," he cried in a high wheezy voice, "I've got the most tremendous piece of news. Fabulous, my dear boy, absolutely fabulous!"

"Good!" Alan showed no sign of catching fire. "Sir Lancelot Telly—Miss Inga Dobb."

She gave him her best smile.

"How de do?" All she had was a mere flicker of a glance; and then, rising above her chagrin, she realized why. Like so many leaders of London's aesthetic and cultural life, Sir Lancelot was not interested in pretty young women, his tastes lying elsewhere; all this appearance of virile tweedy masculinity was a sham. He had in fact, as she saw now, the eyes of an hysterical middle-aged woman.

"Coffee?" asked Alan.

"Good God, no! I don't know how you can drink the stuff. And I'm taking you up to the Policy Meeting in a minute or two. My dear boy, the most fabulous news! I've just heard from the Cultural Attaché of the Norroland Embassy that Stannsen has at last finished his Tenth Symphony—and that *the first performance of it can be given here—*"

"Stannsen's Tenth?" Alan was gaping. "Are you sure, Lancelot?"

"Of course I'm sure. I wouldn't run round announcing a thing like this, if I weren't. The E.B.C. Symphony Orchestra is offered the privilege, the honour, of performing this great work for the first time. And I call it a great work because it's bound to be, you can bet your boots on that."

"I would," cried Alan fervently. He looked at Inga, who was glad to see that he could show some enthusiasm. "You probably know about Stannsen. He's the greatest living composer—"

"Yes, yes, yes," said Inga. "And he's finished his Tenth Symphony at last—and you can play it. But why you?"

"Why not?" Sir Lancelot looked haughty and aggrieved.

"It's a fair question," said Alan. "Why us—for the first performance? Why not his own Norroland chaps—or the Berlin Philharmonic—or the Vienna—or the Boston—or the

Philadelphia—?"

"You're not suggesting I can't do justice to the work, are you?" Sir Lancelot was still annoyed. He was staring haughtily at Alan; apparently Inga had ceased to exist.

"No, I'm not," said Alan. "I'm merely asking—like Miss Dobb—why us?"

"Well, the usual thing—wheels within wheels, of course. I gathered from this Embassy fellow that the President of Norroland's paying an official visit here—to sign a trade agreement or something of that sort—so the idea is for us to give a special concert at the Festival Hall—royalty present and that kind of thing—"

"Ah, now it makes sense. That's fine. Congratulations, Lancelot!"

"Thanks, my dear boy. Now we've got to talk to these fellows upstairs—work up some enthusiasm. There won't be too much time, I gather—so we'll all have to get together on the thing. What's the time? We'd better go."

Inga stood up, and smiled at Alan. As Sir Lancelot had been ignoring her, she now ignored him. "Thank you for being so kind to me, Mr. Applerose." She held out her hand. "I hope the Stannsen concert will be a great success. I suppose if I want to know any more about it, I can always find you here. Good-bye!"

"Good-bye, Miss Dobb! Try again for the poetry reading—but not Mildred next time."

She turned, having already moved away. She was smiling. "By the way—about Stannsen. He happens to be my godfather." And off she went.

Sir Lancelot stared after her. "For a moment I thought she said Stannsen was her godfather. What *did* she say?"

"That he happens to be her godfather."

Sir Lancelot half rose. "Good gracious me—!"

"She's probably lying," said Alan gloomily. "She has a sort of golden pussycat look, the way they do have when they're lying. Trying to impress you, Lancelot—you were very uppish with her. Pity, though—to spoil it like that. Very attractive girl, though too cheeky for my taste. Well, I'll pay for this muck—and we'll go and talk to the heads."

By the time they arrived at the Policy Meeting, Sir Lancelot had begun to sketch an all-Stannsen programme — one of the early tone poems, the Second Symphony or the Piano Concerto — then the long-awaited Tenth, on the air of course as well, with hook-ups all over the place; and, as Alan guessed, had already seen himself receiving some Norroland order, some whacking great gold star with a blue or scarlet ribbon six inches wide. If he could work it, the old boy — known among the instrumentalists as the *Adagio Queen* — would end up looking like a Christmas tree. Still, he was a tolerably good musician, as well as being a first-class showman, and it was pleasant to see him enthusiastic again. After that young Czech violinist fled to America, Lancelot had been depressed and peevish for months; this news was bringing him to life again.

The Policy Meeting had already started. Alan joined it inconspicuously and wished he had a cigar. He was not really an E.B.C. man, and had joined the staff, after doing many odd jobs for them, only when the slump in British film production, which had kept him going since the war, had compelled him to find some regular work. In his own serious composition, he was slow and fastidious, but he could write nonsense stuff with great facility, was an excellent technician, and could rehearse and conduct any possible ensemble. The E.B.C. musicians respected and liked him. He liked them, as he did most of the producers, engineers, sound effects boys and girls, and the rest; but he did not care for the heads of departments and the administrative types, all the sort of people who could be found at Policy Meetings.

The head of the Company, Air Marshal Block, was in the chair. He was a big, dour man, obviously ready to lay waste a dozen cities without batting an eyelid; and no doubt on the highest levels, where his appointment had been made, his ignorance of all forms of culture and his dislike of popular entertainment were all in his favour. At this moment he was wrestling with the problem of *Call It Clumps*, one of the E.B.C.'s parlour games, considered by some sections of the public and press to be one of the Company's triumphs, by others to be a national disaster.

Westfort was talking. He was a donnish type, the metaphysician of Radio Centre. "What I feel, sir, is that now in this programme we're obtaining a higher ratio of identity response. The sharp division of opinion, in my view, sir, is an essential part of that identity response. Depending of course on the individual aggressive factor. Taking Erbach's classification — the Beta type will find it cathartic. The other three types will be more regressive, naturally. In short, sir, I'm asking for a longer-term view of *Call It Clumps —*"

"Humph!" said the Air Marshal, who, being a Strong Man, could make this noise sound quite impressive. "Something in that, Westfort. Yes, Porton?"

"With all due respect, sir," said Porton, who was a Civil Service type, always with a lot of due respect playing both ends against the middle, "I think that unless the listening figure drops badly, we should keep it on another month, and then if there's still so much opposition to it, especially in the press, we should ask the question master, Cragg, who's our man, to drop out, announcing that he needs a rest. The programme won't survive the disappearance of Cragg, I believe, sir. And we shan't appear to have had our hand forced. I'm sure Publicity could handle the situation —"

"Certainly," cried Mamber, who was in charge of Publicity. "Cragg'll play all right. Nobody better. And we need something — though I'm not saying I wouldn't like something bigger and juicier —"

Sir Lancelot, who had been restive ever since his arrival, now made an obviously impatient move, as if to catch the chairman's eye.

"Yes, Telly?" said the Air Marshal. "Got something to say? Not quite your kind of thing, though, is it?"

"Not my kind of thing at all," said Sir Lancelot, who, to give him his due, was always ready to speak his mind on these occasions. "Never understood why people can't play their own idiotic games —"

There were several protests, but the chairman demanded silence for Sir Lancelot.

"Only wanted to say that if Mamber is asking for something better, I can give it to him, with your permission." Sir Lancelot, who had a fine sense of the dramatic, now paused artfully. "I don't want to rush the meeting, Mr. Chairman. But I've very important news — and a good deal to do in connection with it — so as soon as you've finished discussing your Clumps or whatever they are, I'd like to explain what's happened."

The Air Marshal grunted. "Some musical business, I take it. Well, better put us in the picture. Porton, you and Westfort settle this Clumps thing between you. Now then, Telly!"

"The greatest living composer," Sir Lancelot began, forcing himself to speak with the weightiest possible deliberation, "is Stannsen—of Norroland. Am I right, Applerose?"

"Unquestionably," said Alan. He ran the risk of taking too much of the meeting's time by adding, "Absolutely."

"The world," continued Sir Lancelot, holding up his right forefinger, as if about to bring in a whole section of strings, "has been impatiently waiting for Stannsen to finish his Tenth Symphony. Mr. Chairman, now it is finished. Stannsen's Tenth Symphony is ready for its first performance."

"A good thing too, I've no doubt," said the Air Marshal dubiously. "But we'd better get on."

"We *are* getting on," cried Sir Lancelot. "This is the point. The English Broadcasting Company Symphony Orchestra has been given the privilege of offering that performance to the waiting world. That is my news, Mr. Chairman." He looked round haughtily. Even the Air Marshal was impressed. "And if anybody has any more important announcement to make this morning, then for the time being I'll say no more."

Having thus sonorously stated his main subject on the brass, Sir Lancelot now swept the strings and woodwind into a magnificent *allegro*. President of Norroland's official visit— trade agreement—all on highest level—special concert at Royal Festival Hall also on this level—royalty, ministers, decorations and orders—world-wide hook-ups—greatest event of the season from every point of view. To all of which, Mamber, head of Publicity, gave rapturous assent: this was what he had been wanting. Even the Air Marshal began to smoulder with enthusiasm, for although the music itself would probably be torture to him, here was an occasion undoubtedly on the highest level, glittering with V.I.P.s, radiant with orders and decorations, far removed from the suburban squabbles about *Call It Clumps*. For once a smile lit up his heavy face, as a burning university might light up a whole blasted area. "Let's have action on this," he cried, as if a thousand factories were to be destroyed that night. "You fellows get weaving."

They wove up in Sir Lancelot's office, but after a few minutes, when Sir Lancelot and Mamber were fixing up a press conference, Alan saw that he was not needed and returned to his own room. He had another look at the score for *No Unicorns on Thursday*, decided that it really was as bad as he had thought, and began to think about the slow movement of his *Suite for Strings*. Just before one o'clock, Mildred came charging in, still cross. "Well— really—!"

"Yes, Mildred?"

"I was furious with you this morning, Alan. Still am. The way you talked! And bringing that appalling girl in when you knew I was rehearsing! What have you done with her?"

"I haven't done anything with her, Mildred. She was just a girl wandering about the corridor. Rather a cheeky young woman, I admit. She ended up by telling Lancelot that Stannsen's her godfather, just because Lancelot ignored her, being off his head about doing a first performance of Stannsen's Tenth. A mischievous lying wench, I'm afraid."

"I'm not surprised. Well, I must fly. I'm lunching with Edward—"

"Then you can give Edward his chum's *Unicorn* score—"

"Don't be ridiculous, Alan. Of course I can't. You'll have to do something with it."

For some reason that he could not discover, and much to his own surprise, Alan for once was firm with her. "I'm not doing anything with it, except giving it back to you. Here! I don't like these unicorns and seal women, I don't like Edward and his chums, I don't like this score—"

"Why don't you say you don't like me—and have done with it?" She gave him a two-second glare, then was gone, banging the door behind her.

It was then that Alan began to wonder if he really did like her, and why they were supposed to be engaged. Meditating upon this theme, he drifted out of his room and went along to the usual pub, where he drank bitter and ate corned-beef sandwiches in the company of a principal viola, a bassoon and a tenor horn, and Charlie, the cynical pianist. They received with respect the news of Stannsen's Tenth, but Charlie, a low, lecherous type, preferred to discuss Miss Inga Dobb. "Where d'you find 'em, Alan boy? And what's the good of your finding 'em if you don't know what to do with 'em? No telephone number, no address? You'll never compose great music this way, boy. Why—Stannsen would have had her roaring drunk with him by this time. I'll tell you what's the matter with you boys." Which he proceeded to do, using many coarse Anglo-Saxon terms.

# CHAPTER II

# MR. DOBB SAYS NO

A FEW days later, Alan returned to his room at Radio Centre from a rehearsal to find Mrs. Crisp, Sir Lancelot's secretary, waiting for him. She was a large, maternal, Corn Queen sort of woman, always on the look-out for E.B.C. geniuses who needed a woman's care and devotion. As Alan came into this category, he always tried to be very tough with her.

"Where have you been, Alan? Lancelot's screaming for you."

"Both of you appear to have forgotten," Alan told her, "that we have an ensemble here known as *The Twilight Players*, who as dusk descends offer us a few exquisite soothing melodies. It's been my task this morning to conduct a rehearsal of these Twilight Players, who consist of a lot of disgruntled back-desk instrumentalists, smoking pipes, trying to scramble through their exquisite melodies with the least possible effort. What does the *maestro* want?"

"Don't pretend to be so cynical, Alan. I know you're not really like that. The point is—the Stannsen score has arrived. A Viking brought it from the Norroland Embassy—honestly, you'd have thought he was a Viking."

"I wouldn't. I've never seen a Viking. Before my time. However, the Stannsen score—that really ought to be something. Lead on, dear Mrs. Crisp."

Sir Lancelot, seated with the Stannsen score, was swelling like a peacock. "Brought by one of the Embassy officials, my boy. By the way, you've seen all the publicity, have you? I must say, Mamber's doing a very good job. I've been in touch with both the Arts Council and the British Council—all very enthusiastic, of course. And royalty are almost certain, I think. But I'm leaving that to Block. The date's more or less fixed. Stannsen's using a very large orchestra, of course—and naturally it isn't an easy work." The telephone rang. "If that's the press, Mrs. Crisp, say that I'm not to be disturbed as I'm now going through the Stannsen score—a great privilege." He looked proudly at Alan. "I feel I must go through this alone first, my boy. You won't begrudge me that, I imagine. Your time will come, I've no doubt—"

"I have. I'll never make a first-class conductor, and there won't be any more Stannsens. However, if I could go through it when you've finished, Lancelot—"

"Of course. I was about to say that, my dear boy. No, Mrs. Crisp—whoever it is, I mustn't be disturbed. Be firm, be firm. Well, that's all for the moment, Alan. I just wanted you to know it's here. Where've you been, by the way?"

"Rehearsing our Twilight Players in a few exquisite—"

"No, no, no, please! Though I quite understand how you feel. Couldn't Johnson or one of those fellows take them in future? Mrs. Crisp, make a note—if I'm to be up to the neck in this Stannsen, as indeed I must be, then Alan must be taken off that horrible ensemble. No, no—no thanks, my dear boy—it's the least I could do. Oh—another thing. This Stannsen concert means I shan't be able to do your *Suite* this side of Christmas. But I believe you said you were having difficulty with the work. Quite—quite, quite! Well, you shall have a look at this as soon as I've gone through it. Wonderful work—great privilege!" He waved Alan out. "No, Mrs. Crisp. Not even the Air Marshal. I have my responsibilities just as he has his—but don't put it like that."

A little later a message came from Miss Mildred Povey's secretary to say that Miss Povey would be glad if Mr. Applerose could accompany her that night to the New Elizabethan Playhouse to see a performance of *Gammer Gurton's Needle*. To which Mr. Applerose replied that he regretted his inability to attend this performance but, as he had already indicated to Miss Povey, he was engaged that night, having promised to put in an appearance at the Chamber Music Club. Ten minutes and twenty-seven seconds later he received a direct message from Miss Mildred Povey informing him that he was a selfish stinker and this just about tore it. To which Mr. Applerose replied, vaguely but not without a certain admirable firmness, that Miss Povey could please herself but that was how it was. He then returned to his examination of some astonishing music, written for double-bass, two 'cellos, and eight woodwind, designed to add fire and depth to a feature programme about Yugoslavia. He lunched in Soho with a Central European pianist, who had brought with him a madwoman who had written an opera based on Shelley's *Prometheus Unbound*: not a good lunch, and no cigar, and the talk with the pianist and the madwoman was not sprightly. It might be a good idea, he decided as he walked back to Radio Centre, to seek refuge as a lay-brother in a monastery, preferably one in close touch with Havana.

He found Sir Lancelot still closeted with the score, but now wearing an old blue velvet jacket over his yellow waistcoat and drinking brandy-and-ginger-ale. "Never even went out for lunch, my dear boy. Had a tray sent up—good God—what dreadful food! That's why I'm drinking this, for my stomach's sake. Well now—it's a great work—without question a great work. Nothing revolutionary—nothing perhaps strictly new, if you know your Stannsen as I do, but very solid, masterly, very—er—moving. Not easy of course, but everything fairly straightforward, except for a bit of nonsense in the last movement." He found the place in the score. "You see? Even a contra-bassoon couldn't find its way down there."

"It must be a joke," said Alan, staring at the lowest notes he had ever seen in a score.

"Yes, but look at this remark by the composer, who says that these notes, essential to the score, can only be played on a Dobbophone. There you are—read it for yourself. Dobbophone!"

Alan laughed. "I'm sorry, Lancelot—I see you're not amused—but it sounds so ridiculous—"

"Ridiculous? Of course it's ridiculous. What does he think I conduct—a band in a variety act? There isn't such a thing in serious music as a Dobbophone. No, of course it's one of his little jokes—trying to catch us out. Probably put it in while he was drunk—drinks like a fish of course—famous for it even in Norroland, where everybody drinks like a fish. You've been there, of course?"

"Never managed it, Lancelot. Though I've always wanted to meet old Stannsen."

"My dear boy, I was ill for weeks after I came back. It's like being suddenly pitched into a saga. Enormous fellows, broad as they're long, all tossing off bumpers of their variety of schnapps, even stronger than the Swedish or Danish stuff. I thought I saw hundreds of huge green mice come out of the woodwork, the last night I was there. Anyhow, I've sent a message to Stannsen, through the Embassy—quickest way of course, congratulating him on the work and so on and so forth, and telling him that we'll move this passage up and play it on the contra-bassoon. Shouldn't have any difficulty there. He's had his joke. Let's go through the score together, my boy. You may spot one or two things I've missed. Typical Stannsen introduction—rather like the Fourth, of course—"

They were still happily tasting the work when Mrs. Crisp's Viking walked in. Alan knew at once it must be. "Yes, yes, yes," he roared, beaming down upon them, "it is Hafstalman again to trouble you, Sir Lancelot Telly."

"A pleasure, Mr. Hafstalman," said Sir Lancelot in his best Embassy manner. "And may I introduce my assistant, Mr. Alan Applerose?"

The genial monster bowed, then seized Alan's hand and tried to pulp it. Finally he sat down, with a wide display of the largest pair of black-and-grey striped trousers Alan had ever seen. Then, without any encouragement, he roared with laughter, slapping his gigantic knees.

"I have you know a telephone conversation with Dr. Stannsen," he roared. "To give him your message, Sir Lancelot Telly. He is a great man, Dr. Stannsen, but also as you must know he is a very fonny man. In Norroland some of the chokes of Dr. Stannsen are told in all places. Even our peasants know these chokes of Dr. Stannsen."

"I take it, Mr. Hafstalman," said Sir Lancelot rather coldly, "that this introduction of what he is pleased to call the Dobbophone into the symphony is one of Dr. Stannsen's jokes? That is what I imagined, of course. And I assume we have his permission to re-score the passage for contra-bassoon."

"No, please," said Hafstalman, smiling broadly, "it is not so. Dr. Stannsen asked me to tell you those notes are important and must be played as they are written only for the Dobbophone. If no Dobbophone, then no symphony."

"But my dear sir," cried Sir Lancelot, not hiding his exasperation, "that's preposterous. There's no such instrument in my orchestra as a Dobbophone. I've never heard of the thing before. Neither has Mr. Applerose here. Have you?"

"Unless it was used in hunting Snarks," said Alan, who was beginning to enjoy himself.

"Please," said Hafstalman, as Sir Lancelot was about to denounce this levity. "I tell you of this Dobbophone. Just like Dr. Stannsen tells me, of course. It exists, this Dobbophone, here in London. It is special deep bass thing invented by old friend of Dr. Stannsen who lives here in London—Mr. Dobb. For many years Dr. Stannsen and Mr. Dobb are great friends. Then they have quarrel—" Here he began roaring with laughter again, to the obvious annoyance of Sir Lancelot. "I am sorry but this is very fonny, this quarrel, because it is about game of *Strunshka*, which is card game played in Norroland among peasants—"

"Mr. Hafstalman, I'll be delighted at some other time to learn about the sports and pastimes of the Norroland peasantry, with or without any reference to Dr. Stannsen. But I must point out that we're discussing the first performance of a great musical work, which we've already announced to the press—"

"Yes, yes, please, I am sorry, Sir Lancelot Telly." And Hafstalman rose, bowed majestically, then said with some severity, "It is all simple. Dr. Stannsen says he has written a part for Dobbophone and on Dobbophone it must be played. And Mr. Dobb, who invented it and can play it, is here in London. So next you speak with Mr. Dobb." Without another word, he bowed again, whipped out two large invitation cards and gave one to each of them, bowed yet once more, and marched out. The cards invited them to an official luncheon at the Norroland Embassy, the following week; and Alan mentally accepted at once. He was no Embassy type, but he felt he was prepared to make an exception of the Norroland Embassy.

"Dobbophone," Sir Lancelot was muttering as he wandered about the room, looking disgusted. "Did you ever hear of anything so preposterous? Of course I've never heard the instrument—and possibly it may give him something in the bass that he needs—it's just possible, though not very likely. Still, you know what composers are."

"Certainly. I *am* one."

"Very well. I accept that." Sir Lancelot pointed at him. "Would you demand a Dobbophone—whatever that is? Of course you wouldn't—"

"I might if I were Stannsen—"

"I don't believe *any* instrument can play those notes—"

"He's the best judge of that, Lancelot. He heard his chum Dobb trying it out, before and after they played—what was it?—*Strunshka*—"

"My God, Alan, you're nearly as bad as that Nordic outsize moron who calls himself a Cultural Attaché. Now drop it, that's a good fellow. There are times these days when I feel I'm going out of my mind."

"I'm with you there, Lancelot."

"Here we are, with everything being set up on the very highest level, with everybody waiting to hear what we make of this work," cried Sir Lancelot, glaring round the room as if at some restless, noisy audience, "and what happens?"

"Dobbophone and *Strunshka*," said Alan with relish.

"And what are they?" demanded Mamber, who came rushing in at that moment. Mamber had once been a New York correspondent of a London daily, and he modelled himself on the newspapermen of Hollywood films. He ran his work on manic-depressive lines; he was either too gloomy and lethargic to put out the shortest paragraph about anything or went rushing about, crazily enthusiastic, half drunk with excitement and double gins.

"Tell him, Alan. I must go and wash." And Sir Lancelot took a towel and sponge bag and stalked out.

"Don't tell me it's all off." Mamber was genuinely alarmed.

"No. But Stannsen's asking us to play the lowest bass notes ever put down on paper. And they need something called a Dobbophone." He went on to explain the Dobbophone situation. Mamber listened entranced.

"I don't care what Lancelot feels about it," cried Mamber, "but this is a fabulous break for my boys and girls. I tell you, it's beginning to have everything. I've dreamt stories like this. *Dobb's Great Chance. Musical Inventor Saves New Symphony. Who is Dobb?* Just add the sex angle, and it's all there—"

"Perhaps Dobb'll turn out to be a beautiful twenty-year-old

girl," Alan began rather sourly. Then he stared at Mamber.

"You've got something. What is it? Give—give!"

"There was a girl here the other day called Dobb. Probably a coincidence. But she said Stannsen was her godfather. I thought she was lying. Probably she was."

"How was she on looks?"

Alan had to think for a moment. "She was all right. Very pretty, in fact. A dazzling blonde."

"That's all we need—a dazzling blonde—and then this story really has everything. Now, Alan, promise me that if this girl comes into it, let me know at once. Got her phone number or address? No? Don't work very fast, do you?"

"In that sense," Alan replied with dignity, "I don't work at all."

Sir Lancelot came back, looking as clean and pink as a baby. "I've just remembered that I have to rehearse that dreadful young woman with the bangles in the Tschaikowsky B Flat Minor," he announced bitterly. "What's the use of pretending that the British public's taste improves, when I conduct more performances of that damned work now than I did thirty years ago? And the pianists were better too then. No young women with bangles. Well, Alan my boy, I must leave this wretched Dobb business to you. Go and see him—make sure he can play the instrument—and then tell him that at the special request of the composer, he'll have the privilege of playing at our special Stannsen concert. I hope there won't be any trouble with the Musicians' Union," he added gloomily. "There usually is. After the rehearsal I shall go home. I've had quite enough of this building for one day. Good-day, gentlemen!" And off he went.

"That's all very well," cried Alan. "But all I know about this Dobb is that he invented something called the Dobbophone, used to know Stannsen and quarrelled with him over a game of cards. I don't know his other name, where he lives, or anything."

"I'll get my secretary on to it," said Mamber, and told her over the telephone to track down a man called Dobb, probably an inventor and not likely to be a young man. He spent the next ten minutes explaining to Alan, who was not interested, what plans for further publicity he had in mind. "And don't forget," he said in conclusion, "you've got to co-operate, for all our sakes."

"I'll do what I'm expected to do," said Alan, "what I'm paid to do, and that's all, Mamber. I don't enjoy these publicity games. I'm tired of seeing people being got at. I wish they could be left alone—"

"They'd die of boredom, half of 'em, nowadays."

"All right. Let 'em die of boredom. If people need these stunts to keep 'em alive, they aren't fit to live. No, I'm serious, Mamber. I think people these days are spoilt in the wrong way. Everything's doctored to appeal to their idiotic tastes and prejudices."

"Don't you want 'em to know about Stannsen's new symphony, Alan? Come now."

"It looks a fine work. Stannsen's a great man. But I don't want it and him all spiced and jazzed up just to tickle this idiot mob."

"I hope you're not going to talk like that to Dobb—"

"No, I'm not, naturally. I'll take Lancelot's line—it's a great privilege for him to take part in our big show."

Mamber's secretary came through to say that the man they wanted must be Roland Dobb, who had a very brief entry in *Who's Who*, where he appeared as "an inventor". He was born in 1886, which suggested that he belonged to Stannsen's generation. He lived at 9 Marlin Gardens, Hampstead. No telephone number was given in *Who's Who*, and his name was not in the Telephone Directory.

"Evidently a cagey old boy," said Mamber. "Would you like me to go with you?"

"No. All wrong. He should be approached by the Music Department and not by Publicity. I suppose I'd better see him to-day if I can."

"Don't do that, old man. Wait till morning."

"Why?"

Mamber had evidently come to some notable decision. His eyes, a bloodshot grey, glittered. "I'm going to let the story break to-night—so he'll read about himself to-morrow morning."

"Probably he doesn't read the sort of papers that'll print your story—"

"No harm done if he doesn't. Besides, you can take them with you just to show him what's happening. He'll leap at it, you'll see. I must get busy. Have I got all the dope? Now, let's just check. There's a bit in this piece specially written for a Dobbophone, invented by Dobb, an old friend of Stannsen's who won't allow his symphony to be played if there's any tampering with these low, low notes. Am I right? I'll pass the word along to the boys, then. And, Alan, the minute you get back from seeing him in the morning, let me know. You wouldn't like to take a photographer along, would you?"

"Certainly not. I'm the Assistant Musical Director of the E.B.C. going to talk to an instrumentalist—I don't cart photographers about with me."

"Dead right, old man. The wrong approach. Well, let me have the story in the morning—hot, strong, and pronto."

It was about half-past ten next morning when Alan, carrying half a dozen different newspapers that featured Mamber's story of Dobb and the Stannsen Symphony, walked briskly along Marlin Gardens, Hampstead. He did not walk briskly because he was eager to meet Mr. Dobb but because there was already a bite in the October air, he was wearing his thin suit, and at the last moment had not been able to find his overcoat. The houses in Marlin Gardens were tall and thin and nervously baroque; each had a neglected bit of soil in front and steep steps running up to the door. It was very, very quiet round there, probably waiting, Alan thought, for all the Central European tenants of the flats and maisonnettes to return from their consulting rooms, publishers' offices, antique shops, wholesale novelty warehouses. Number Nine did not look as bad as some of its neighbours, only rather careless. Just as Alan was about to ring the bell, a middle-aged woman came out. She was carrying a shopping basket and wore a rakish purple hat that seemed to belong to somebody else.

"Yes, Mr. Dobb *is* in. Second floor front's his own special room, an' that's where he is. Talkin' to someone, but if I was you I'd go straight up, otherwise he'll take no notice even if you ring an' ring. Not yuman, I call it, just not botherin' like that, but that's how he is, Mr. Dobb. So you just go straight up an' in, only don't tell him I told you. Do you know Mr. Dobb?"

Alan had to admit that he did not know Mr. Dobb.

"You're not tryin' to sell him anythink, are you?"

"No, I'm not. In fact, I've never sold anybody anything. I'm a musician."

"Oh—that'll be all right, then. I thought you didn't have the look of them salesmen. Well, Mr. Dobb in some ways is as nice a gentleman as ever breathed—but then in other ways he's a terror. An' you never know which it'll turn out to be." In her deepest heart, woman wants man to be incalculable; and now beneath the horrible purple hat there appeared a smile of the purest female appreciation. "Makes it interestin', not knowin' like, as I tell my husband when he says I don't need to come out an' oblige. Well, you go straight up—"

"Thank you. By the way, have you read any of the papers this morning?"

"Don't have my read till afternoon. Mr. Dobb, he doesn't take any papers—"

"I see. Thank you very much."

"It's a pleasure, I'm sure." She seemed to feel that they had had quite a nice little party on the doorstep; and perhaps they had.

The interior of Number Nine was like its exterior, not quite neglected and run-down, but careless. When he reached the first landing, Alan could hear voices from the floor above. Climbing the second flight of stairs, he caught the fragrance of good cigar smoke, and sniffed ecstatically. Somebody—and he could only hope it was Mr. Dobb—was smoking an uncommonly fine cigar—and at this hour in the morning too. Among Alan's visions was one of himself lighting an eight-inch Havana at about this time, and now the light that he saw through the open door of the second-floor front room seemed touched with a visionary gleam. He walked towards it, making as much noise as possible. There was no point in knocking on the door because by the time he reached it he could be clearly seen—and was.

"Mr. Dobb? I'm sorry to barge in like this—but I couldn't make anybody hear—"

"Are you selling anything, young man?"

"No. As a matter of fact, I'm a musician—"

"Come in, then, come in," said Mr. Dobb. His lined, leathery face and coarse, untidy grey hair suggested his age; but his restless and gleaming eyes still had youth in them; and he was wearing a sort of lumberman's shirt and an old corduroy jacket that gave him a pioneering look. Nobly decorating the right-hand corner of his wide mouth, burning evenly in the blue air of Paradise, was the Havana of Alan's dreams. And perhaps he noticed Alan's wistful glance. "Have a cigar?"

"Oh—could I?" cried Alan, forgetting himself, like a child of ten.

"Now—at last—here's a man who likes a cigar." Mr. Dobb held out the box, from which Alan plucked, as a boy in a fairy tale might pluck an apple of gold, an eight-inch Havana of a noble brand. "That's why you and I can't understand each other."

This was said to a quivering little man in dark clothes who was sitting on the edge of his chair. However, he was not without spirit. "I'm only too anxious to reach an understanding, Mr. Dobb. But not at the risk of poisoning myself with nicotine. Besides, I don't like cigars."

"Well said, Mr. Primpton." He looked at Alan. "What's your name?"

"Applerose."

Mr. Dobb frowned. "I've heard that name—just lately too. However, don't let's bother about that. This is my accountant, Mr. Primpton. Just enjoy that cigar while we finish our talk."

Alan asked for nothing better. It was the finest cigar that had come his way for some time. He was sitting in an old-fashioned rocking-chair, and now he rocked gently as the other two began talking, and gazed dreamily through the smoke, the entrancing haze of Cuba. The room was actually a rather large one but seemed small because there was so little vacant space in it. Round the three walls and beneath the broad window were tables piled with note-books, blue-prints, mysterious little gadgets, all higgledy-piggledy. The walls were covered with maps, plans, large photographs.

An old bureau in one corner was heaped high with cigar boxes. Here, obviously, Mr. Dobb did his inventing, aided by the noblest exports of Cuba and Jamaica.

"But, Mr. Dobb," the little man was protesting, "all I'm trying to do is to keep you out of trouble. You must see, they'll soon be down on you like a ton of bricks."

"I've had a ton of bricks down on me. It's overrated. The question is, Primpton, are you on my side or theirs?"

"No, no, no, Mr. Dobb—please! That's not the question at all. I've pleaded and pleaded with your Tax Inspector, pointing out that you've spent so much time abroad, that you've earned a great deal of foreign currency, that you're so busy with your inventions and so absent-minded—"

"Then I'm ashamed of you, Primpton. I'm not at all absent-minded—"

"But I must tell them *something*. I can't tell them you refuse to pay your taxes because you want to buy cigars—"

"Why not?"

"Because—why—I mean to say—one couldn't possibly talk to them like that—it just isn't—"

As poor little Mr. Primpton went floundering on, Alan examined Mr. Dobb with renewed interest and respect. Undoubtedly this was the magnificent uncle to whom Miss Inga Dobb had referred, for there could not be two Dobbs who refused to pay taxes because they preferred to buy cigars. This was the glorious rebel himself.

"I'm a reasonable man," Mr. Dobb was saying. "And it seems to me I'm adopting a reasonable attitude. Here am I, in my sixties, still working away, hoping to improve the human lot. I like good cigars. They are now a fantastic price, about fifteen times what they were when I first began buying them. And why? Chiefly because the Government has raised the duty on them to a monstrous height. But I pay this duty—I don't smuggle in my cigars, though I've sometimes thought of it. In fact, I give the Government about ten times as much as its activities are worth to me, and was prepared to accept this without complaint. But you and these fellows come along and tell me I must pay so much in direct taxation that I wouldn't have enough left to buy a few decent cigars. I'm told, in fact, to change the habit of a lifetime— told by a Treasury whose First Lord is apparently never seen in public without a first-class Havana—"

"He must get them given," cried Mr. Primpton. "Please, Mr. Dobb—be sensible—"

"Sensible!" Mr. Dobb thundered. "What the devil do you mean? I *am* being sensible. It's you fellows who are being idiotic. If the Treasury will arrange for me to have a constant free supply of good cigars, then I'll pay them the equivalent in direct taxation. If they'll leave me alone, I'll go on supplying them with a handsome revenue out of the duty on cigars."

"You must know that's quite impossible, Mr. Dobb," Mr. Primpton moaned. "You're legally bound to pay income-tax and surtax—"

"I don't consider myself under any obligation to pay for things I don't want and entirely disapprove of. For example," and Mr. Dobb pointed an accusing finger, "I understand that the Government is spending a great deal of money on atom bombs and all that sort of thing. Now, I've never been asked if I consented, and if I had been asked, I would have said at once that it was ruinous folly for this country to enter the race for atomic armaments. But the people who tell me they need every penny I can scrape together are the very people who, without asking my permission, have committed themselves—and me—to this extravagant idiocy. I am to go without cigars so that they can play with atom bombs. I doubt if the maddest Oriental despots ever made such demands. And it's the final impertinence to call this form of government a democracy. Sheer tyranny! Our forefathers, Primpton, wouldn't have put up with it for a single week—"

The little man jumped up. "What's the use of talking like that, Mr. Dobb? The men I have to see aren't interested in such arguments—"

"Then send them to me," said Dobb. "Drop the whole business, my dear fellow. I can see you're very unhappy about it. Tell them you're out of it and they must deal directly with me."

"Very well, Mr. Dobb. But you'll get into trouble."

"Don't worry about me. I enjoy getting into a certain amount of trouble. Now off you go—and tell that fellow to come and argue with *me*." He accompanied Mr. Primpton to the landing, patting him on the back.

This gave Alan time to consider how he would persuade this formidable man to play his Dobbophone. Sir Lancelot's rather condescending approach—here was a chance for Dobb to distinguish himself—seemed less promising than ever. Tact would be needed. And nobody yet had ever commended Alan Applerose for his tact.

"A musician, eh?" said Mr. Dobb immediately on his return. "Composer?"

Alan nodded and smiled.

"Excellent! I'm very fond of music—always have been. A young composer who likes a good cigar—that's a promising start." Mr. Dobb made himself comfortable. "What can I do for you?"

"I must explain," said Alan rather reluctantly, "that at present I'm Assistant Musical Director of the English Broadcasting Company—"

Mr. Dobb had a most expressive face, and what it expressed now offered Alan no encouragement to continue.

"So really I'm representing the Musical Director—Sir Lancelot Telly—"

"I'm sorry to hear it. The man's a charlatan. He ought to be selling millinery, not conducting Beethoven and Brahms."

Alan tried to look as if he had not heard these remarks. "Stannsen has finished his Tenth Symphony and we're to give the first performance of it." He hurried on. "The score's arrived—and there's a short passage in the last movement that Stannsen says must be played on your Dobbophone—"

"Oh—he does, does he?"

"He insists. So Sir Lancelot asked me to tell you how delighted he'd be if you'd play your instrument for us at our special Stannsen concert. You haven't seen the papers, have you?"

"I haven't seen the papers," said Mr. Dobb grimly. "And I don't want to see the papers."

"Well, the President of Norroland is paying an official visit—and he'll attend this concert—and possibly royalty and political bigwigs—the whole thing's being done on the highest possible level. I suppose, Mr. Dobb, you still have the instrument and can still play it—"

"As a matter of fact, I have—and I can. But go on—go on."

But Alan did not feel like going on. "Well, there it is. Er—Sir Lancelot—"

"Don't let's have any more of this *Sir Lancelot* stuff," cried Mr. Dobb. "Sounds as if we're trying to recite *The Idylls of the King*. Call him Telly."

"Certainly. Telly feels you'll realize what a privilege—" Alan stopped, then changed direction hastily.

"It's a magnificent work—and of course everybody's longing to hear it. So I hope you'll help us with this first performance,

Mr. Dobb."

"Applejohn—" Mr. Dobb began severely.

But even at these moments of crisis we insist upon our own names. "Applerose."

"Applerose, then. You can go back to Telly and inform him that I've no intention of playing my Dobbophone for him. And if all the crowned heads and presidents in the world were going to be there, I wouldn't play it."

"Mr. Dobb," said Alan desperately, "you can't let us down. I shouldn't have stressed the V.I.P. nonsense—that's Telly's influence. But think about the music—"

"Nonsense! When I tried to persuade Stannsen to write for the Dobbophone, he always refused. Why do you think he's doing it now? I'll tell you. Have you ever played a card game called *Strunshka*? Ah—I see you've heard of it? Well, it's a footling game—but, being an intelligent man, I play it very well when I give my mind—or part of my mind—to it. Now Stannsen and I used to play this game—and sometimes he was lucky. But the last time we played, some years ago, I beat him, but he took advantage of some rule that I'd never heard of before, and that I'll swear he invented, to escape defeat. We had a quarrel—he's an aggressive, hot-tempered fellow, not like me—and I told him there and then that unless he apologised and admitted defeat, our friendship was at an end. There's a limit even to my patience, Applejohn, and he'd passed it. I had—still have—the highest admiration for Stannsen's musical genius, but that's no reason why I should submit to being cheated and bullied. I'm a quiet, patient, unassuming man," roared Mr. Dobb, glaring at Alan like a wounded lion, "but I'm nobody's doormat. Stannsen can't behave like a spoilt child—can't pickle himself in Norroland schnapps and start his antics—and expect me to go back on my word. Let him apologise. Or—I'll stretch a point—let him beat me fairly at *Strunshka* for ten thousand *dumkas*."

"It's Applerose, not Applejohn," Alan shouted. "And what the blazes are *dumkas*?"

Mr. Dobb somehow contrived to look reproachful. "No need to shout, you know, Applerose. Let's talk like two quiet, reasonable men. The *dumka* is the unit of scoring in *Strunshka*. A ten-thousand-*dumka* game lasts between eight and twelve hours. I'll explain the game, if you like. We might just play for a hundred *dumkas*." And he got up.

Alan jumped up at once. "Mr. Dobb, I haven't the time to bother about *Strunshka*. You must realize there's going to be a tremendous fuss if you refuse to play your Dobbophone for us. The story's in the press already." And he held out his collection of morning papers.

"Do you mean to tell me," said Mr. Dobb, outraged, "that these wretched, drivelling newspapers are writing about Stannsen and me?" He snatched the papers from Alan and glanced at them in disgust, throwing them down as he finished with each one. "Good God! Can't they find anything better to write about? It's as I thought. We're within sight of the end of civilization."

It was at that moment that Miss Inga Dobb entered the room. She was followed by a thin, wriggling man, who had a predatory nose, sharp little eyes, and a most ungentlemanly green-striped suit. "Uncle," she cried, "I met Mr. Fettle outside so I brought him up. Oh—you've seen the papers." Then she noticed Alan, and gave him a dazzling glance and smile. "Hello, Mr. Applerose! How nice to see you again! This is Mr. Fettle."

"Pleased to meet," cried Mr. Fettle, with an extra wriggle.

"All right, Joe," said Mr. Dobb, throwing down the last of the papers. "I'm coming along." He turned to Alan. "No Dobbophone."

"Oh uncle!" cried Miss Dobb reproachfully.

"Inga, if this is the young man you described in such handsome terms—"

"I didn't—"

"You can now entertain him at your leisure," Mr. Dobb continued. "But I want both of you to understand that I don't propose to play my Dobbophone at this concert. Come along, Joe."

"Till next time," cried Mr. Fettle, and vanished with Mr. Dobb.

"Now I can give you some coffee," said Miss Dobb, "and it'll be much better than yours—you'll see."

"Thanks. But I mustn't stay too long. You haven't a telephone, have you? No, I thought not. Well, I'll just have a quick cup. I need *something*. There's going to be a hell of a fuss about this Dobbophone business."

"Yes, isn't there?" said Miss Dobb brightly. "It's up in the attic. Would you like to have a look at it while I'm making the coffee. I'll show you. Come on."

She stood at the door of the large gloomy attic, crowded with mysterious dusty objects, pointed the thing out to him, then hurried downstairs. He approached the monster, which was about seven feet high, painted black, and looked as if a more sinister type of Sousaphone had been grafted on to an unusually large contra-bass bassoon. Moving it gingerly, he found the mouthpiece, took a deep breath, and bent down to blow. Nothing happened. He tried again, this time depressing one of the keys he discovered. The sound he produced might have come from the liner *Queen Mary* in a death agony. And something went, as something was bound to go.

"What was that?" cried Miss Dobb, breathless in the doorway.

"The Dobbophone," said Alan gloomily.

"I know that—but the other noise?"

"The top window's gone. However, it was cracked, I noticed."

"Well, come down and have your coffee. Hurry up. What's the matter?"

"I put my cigar down somewhere," said Alan, peering and poking about. "I hope the Dobbophone didn't blow it out of the window. No, it's here."

After she had given him some coffee, she sat down and looked at him as if he were a beautiful present just out of its tissue paper. She was a remarkably beautiful girl, with a real curly mouth of her own and dimples. "You're not quite as dark as I've been thinking you were. Not that I mind," she added hastily.

"You're right about the coffee. Excellent."

"What did I tell you? Are you still half engaged to that awful Mildred?"

"I'm not sure. We're not on the best of terms just now."

"Good! I'm sorry about Uncle Roland. I'm afraid he's going to be rather troublesome. He is, sometimes. The great thing is to stand up to him. Did you stand up to him?"

"Not too well," Alan confessed. "But then I can't help seeing his point of view. Who was Mr. Fettle? He looked a spiv."

"He is a spiv—a sort of king spiv. He's rather sweet really. I don't know what he and Uncle are up to—some secret spivvery, I think. Would you like to take me out to lunch?"

"No, I wouldn't."

"Because of Mildred?"

"Not a bit. Because it costs too much—I don't believe in cheap restaurants; I eat either in pubs or good restaurants—and I haven't time."

"Would you like to come out tonight with me and a girl called Moira who has a lisp and does woodcuts?"

"No. I'm trying to get on with my *Suite for Strings*. Besides, I don't like three, even when nobody has a lisp. And I really must be going now. They're all waiting for the news at Radio Centre."

"Your best plan," said Inga earnestly, "is to keep in touch with me. I think I'd better come down tomorrow morning and tell you what's happening at this end. Would you like another of Uncle Roland's cigars?"

"I would indeed."

"That's the first time I've seen any signs of enthusiasm in you," she told him severely. "I may bring you one tomorrow. It depends how I feel about you."

# CHAPTER III

# THE STORY BREAKS

"LET'S FACE it," cried Sir Lancelot, waddling down the room like an infuriated duck and then turning dramatically, "you've bungled this, Alan. Yes, yes—my fault possibly—you weren't the man for the job. I didn't feel I ought to go myself, because, after all, the conductor of the E.B.C. Orchestra can't go chasing an instrumentalist all over London. But perhaps in this case I ought to have made an exception— Yes, Mrs. Crisp?"

"It's the British Council. They've had a message from the Japanese Embassy—"

"Not now, not now. Later, tell them, later. You see." And he looked accusingly at Alan. "That's the fifth time the British Council has been through already today. To say nothing of the Foreign Office, and the Arts Council of course. *And* the entire press. The truth is, my dear fellow, you bungled it. Instead of explaining properly to this fellow what was expected of him, giving him some notion of the importance of the occasion, you muttered something about his playing his wretched Dobbophone for us—and of course he refused. You say you tried the instrument."

"Just for a moment. One note, actually. It's very rum, of course, but a genuine instrument. Probably not difficult to play."

"He didn't show it to you himself?"

"No, he'd gone out then. His niece showed it to me—the girl you ignored so rudely the other morning in the canteen, Lancelot. The one who said she—"

"Yes, yes, yes. Don't let's waste valuable time."

Mrs. Crisp looked in again. "Mr. Mamber's office *insists* on speaking to him."

"I know what it is," cried Mamber, not for the first time. "And I can't say anything. Tell 'em to hold everything—say they can't find me. Lancelot, you and I'll go and see this chap—"

"It'll probably save time in the end," said Sir Lancelot. "I'll try a musical approach first—ask to see the instrument and that sort of thing—"

"Let's go, then." He grinned at Alan. "What d'you bet we don't persuade him to play it for us?"

"Five pounds," said Alan. "You too, Lancelot. Five pounds you don't. Even though you don't bungle it."

"You can't afford it, my boy. But it's a bet. You have the address, Mamber? Then we're off. Alan, you and Mrs. Crisp can hold the fort here."

"I'm not holding any forts, Lancelot. Otherwise, you'll tell me I've muttered again and bungled it with the Foreign Office, the British Council, the Arts Council, the Press Council, the Privy Council and the London County Council. I'm going back to my room to re-score that accompaniment to the ramble through Yugoslavia. And it's five pounds each you don't bring it off—remember."

Alan spent half an hour on the Yugoslavian score, then broke off to jot down a magnificent second subject for his slow movement, only to realize that Schubert had thought of it first. He was then visited by Porton, the Civil Service type, who came creeping in to make a little quiet mischief.

"I gather this Dobb business is creating quite a stir, Applerose. Surely Mamber was rather premature with his publicity—um? I gather Telly was blaming you. In fact, the Air Marshal as good as told me so. Telly doesn't show much loyalty to his own department, does he? I've noticed that before. The artistic temperament, probably. Between ourselves, Applerose, some of us aren't too happy about Telly, as you probably know."

"I'm not happy about anybody or anything," said Alan, who disliked Porton and all his mysterious intrigues, winks and nudges. He knew that Porton would probably report this—"Applerose isn't happy, you know, and goes about saying so"—partly out of a sheer love of mischief, partly because he had probably somebody in mind for Alan's job, just as he had for Sir Lancelot's. But Alan did not care. "There's just too much fuss about everything—the wrong kind, dam' silly fuss. Why don't we all keep quiet for a change?"

"Quiet," said Porton, eyeing Alan speculatively. "Still, it would hardly do if the English Broadcasting Company kept quiet, would it?"

"It'ud be wonderful," said Alan recklessly. "Do people a world of good. Nothing to switch on for a month. Silence every night. Do them good, do us good."

Porton smiled narrowly. "You'd hardly want me to bring that up at a Policy Meeting as your suggestion, Applerose. But I'm interrupting something, I see." He looked meaningly at the scores on the desk.

"With all due respect, you are, Porton. It may turn out to be something for our Twilight Players to render sweetly in the gloaming. But I hope not."

"A pity. Do you know the listening figures for that programme, Applerose?"

"Yes. Think of a number and then double it. Now I'll give you a bit of gossip to be going on with. I've bet Lancelot and Mamber a fiver each that they don't persuade Dobb to play for us."

"Indeed! That's interesting—ve-ery interesting. Well, I'll let you get on with your work—if it *is* work."

Alan wished he had a cigar. Then he remembered half a broken cheroot he had tossed into a drawer, found it after some difficulty, and under its influence let himself drift away from immediate reality. First, he conducted the Philharmonia in the *allegro* movement of his *Suite for Strings*; next he rehearsed the Vienna Philharmonic in his *Overture to Macbeth*; then he retired to a small tropical island to write his *Concerto for String Quartet and Orchestra,* his most ambitious project; but there appeared unsummoned in the hut where he was working a dazzlingly fair companion, wearing two square feet of scarlet cotton and a few white flowers, and this apparition looked hazily but disturbingly like Miss Inga Dobb....

Reality broke into the room, to his disgust. Two people were grinning at him, delighted with themselves. One was a bold-eyed youngish woman, carrying a fiddle case; the other a fat, untidy, middle-aged man, covered with cigarette ash and dandruff, who flourished a trombone case. They were not E.B.C. instrumentalists.

"Press, old man. Had to borrow these to see you." The man indicated the instrument cases. "I'm Bert Dimmock of the *Record*— and this impudent wench is Helen Mick of the *Morning Star.* We've just come from Dobb's place."

"You really *are* attractive," cried Miss Mick, who had been staring hard. "The girl was quite right."

"What girl?" said Alan.

"The little Dobb girl—the blonde poppet—"

"Nothing doing up there, old man," said Dimmock. "When we left, Sir Lancelot Telly and Pete Mamber hadn't been able to get in to see Dobb. But Helen here caught the niece. About fifty reporters and photographers there already, old man. Climbing all over the place. But Dobb won't let 'em in. So I thought I'd get your story."

"What's the angle on the Dobb girl, Mr. Applerose? Are you in love?" Miss Mick gave him a bold, sweet smile.

"Certainly not," cried Alan. "And there isn't an angle. Please go away."

"Have a heart, old man. What's this *Strunshka* business? Somebody said it's a card game. Where does a card game come into this musical thing?"

"If that girl's not in love with you," said Miss Mick, "I ought to be writing City notes. Don't you know about love, Mr. Applerose? What a waste!"

"Turn it up, Helen," said her colleague severely. "You're making him blush. You women have no shame. Now, old man, you saw Dobb this morning, I understand. What's he like? How did he strike you? Why won't he play this thing-um-bob—Dobbophone?"

"The girl says her uncle and Stannsen had a row," said Miss Mick. "But I never trust these sweet little blondes. They'll say anything for tuppence. Now *you're* different, Mr. Applerose. I'll print anything *you* say. Those steady deep-set eyes do it, though I won't say they haven't let me down before today. Now, Mr. Applerose—*please*!"

"You really ought to talk to Sir Lancelot Telly or Mamber," said Alan, anxious to be rid of these two pests. "All I can tell you is that I saw Mr. Dobb this morning and that he definitely refused to play the part written for the Dobbophone in the Stannsen symphony."

"We know that, old man—"

"Be nice, dear Mr. Applerose—"

They were interrupted by the arrival of one Dr. Grenf, a melancholy Central European character who was musical correspondent for a Continental news agency and often picked up small items from Alan. But it was obvious at once that Dr. Grenf was not acting in his usual modest capacity; here was a chance, not to be missed, of sending some long, exciting cables; he could make some real money at last.

"Dr. Abbleroze," he began, for in his world everybody had received a doctorate, "dees Stannsen story of de Tenth Symvony an' dees beeg bass inzdromend, I think, ees a vondervul story vor my agency an' all my babers on de Condinend. Zo I com' to you, my vrend—"

"Take it easy, old man," cried Dimmock. "We're the press too. British press, old man."

"Are you muzigal gorrespondend? No," Dr. Grenf shouted. "I am muzigal gorrespondend—well known by Dr. Abbleroze, who ees my vrend—"

"Live and let live, though, old man—"

"You gom' here vor muzigal stories? No," Dr. Grenf shouted. "Alvays—many years—I get dees stories. Now ees beeg story—for all babers—so I have sbecial right for brioridy. Yes—brioridy."

"What's he mean—brioridy?" asked Miss Mick.

"Thinks he ought to have priority," said Dimmock.

"Yes—brioridy—brioridy," Dr. Grenf was sweating with anxiety and indignation. He shook his fist, yellow and gnarled from years of exile, at the other two. Then all three of them were shouting.

"For God's sake," Alan yelled, "shut up!"

Into the reproachful silence there entered, smiling with maternal charm, Mrs. Crisp. "Alan, Sir Lancelot's back—and he told me to tell you he's holding a press conference in the drawing-room. In about ten minutes."

"There you are," said Alan, waving the journalists away from his desk, "that's what you want. Press conference. The latest news. Straight from the highest level. Now off you go." And off they went.

Alan waited about twenty minutes, however, before he followed them down to the drawing-room. He was anxious not to be there when the conference began. Once Lancelot had got into his stride— and he was apt to find the press heady company—it was unlikely that Alan would be called upon to say anything. He walked downstairs slowly, loitering to make sure he would not be too early. The drawing-room was not well-named; it was very large, impersonal, dreary, and looked as if it might serve as a waiting-room for some giant dentist.

There were at least fifty journalists of all kinds listening to Sir Lancelot, who was, as Alan saw at once, intoxicated by their presence but concealed this intoxication behind an appearance of immense grandeur and hauteur.

"Certainly, my dear sir," Sir Lancelot was shouting, "that is our intention. We shall perform the work at our special Stannsen concert next month, during the visit of the President of Norroland. If Mr. Dobb persists in this extraordinary decision not to play, that is his look-out. No doubt Stannsen would prefer to hear the passage in the last movement played by his former friend, Mr. Dobb—and, as you know, we are doing everything possible to meet his wishes in this matter—but I cannot believe for a moment that, having offered us the work, he would withdraw his permission, ask us to cancel this very special concert in his honour, merely because Mr. Dobb—who is not himself a musician—chooses to take this—er—extremely unco-operative and, indeed, I might say, unpatriotic attitude. I can assure you that—Dobb or no Dobb—the English Broadcasting Company Symphony Orchestra will perform Stannsen's Tenth Symphony—"

Gloomily Alan listened to this pompous stuff and watched the reporters scribbling away. As he feared, Lancelot was making an ass of himself. It was idiotic to commit the E.B.C. in this fashion. And now somebody asked if Stannsen had not definitely insisted upon the Dobbophone being in the orchestra.

"He objected to the passage being re-scored," cried Sir Lancelot, not quite as grand and haughty as he had been before. "And of course was well within his rights in doing so. I have no doubt whatever that this short passage of exceptionally low notes contributes something to the rich orchestration of the last movement. I have the highest respect for Stannsen's genius, ladies and gentlemen. These notes, though well outside the range of the familiar bass instruments, shall be played as written. Did somebody ask *What on*? Well, let us hope—on the Dobbophone. But if the inventor of that instrument persists in his refusal, then if necessary I will find some other instrument that has the necessary range. I cannot believe that even Mr. Dobb is indispensable—"

"He says he is." This came from a young man who seemed to have just arrived. He was an impudent-looking fellow in an old blue raincoat.

"Indeed!" Sir Lancelot was very haughty now. "And how do you know, my dear sir?"

"Tewson of the *Post*," Alan heard Mamber whisper. "Very hot."

"Because I've just been talking to him." And Tewson looked round at his astonished colleagues, and grinned triumphantly. There were some cries of disbelief. "Take it easy, boys. I've already phoned my story in. Now I'm giving you dead-beats a break."

"Go on, Tewson, you couldn't get in," somebody shouted. "We all tried."

"You didn't try hard enough. We have to be tough on the *Post*. I borrowed a bag of tools and got in as an electrician. Of course he soon tumbled to me and then kicked me out, but not before I'd asked a few questions —"

"What did he say, old man?" Probably Dimmock.

"Read the *Post*, old man. But he certainly thinks he's indispensable."

"Then he's wrong." After fretting at this interruption, Sir Lancelot took charge again. "There are other exceptionally deep bass instruments of this sort — I've heard of several being tried abroad — and if it should be necessary to use one of them, you may be sure we shall do so. I have been entrusted with the first performance of this great work, and I shall play it on the date we have already chosen. And that is my last word, ladies and gentlemen. Thank you!" And he hurried through the nearest door, hastily followed by Mamber and some of his staff, and less hurriedly by Alan.

"But don't forget," Alan told the pair of them upstairs in Sir Lancelot's room, "you owe me a fiver each. You never even set eyes on Dobb. And don't try to change the subject until you've paid me. Come on now. You accused me of bungling, so I'm not going to let you off." And he stood over them, with a hand outstretched, until he was ten pounds richer.

"I shall include it in expenses," said Mamber. "The Company ought to be grateful we didn't see him. Why? Good God! — look at the publicity we'll get now. You couldn't buy it for ten thousand pounds. Headlines all over the world — you watch. Doesn't matter to me whether you play this stuff on a Dobbophone or a banjo, but this is turning out a whale of a story. And, with any luck, it's just beginning. Dobb's only to keep it up, and we may be all set for weeks. Only — now listen, Lancelot, this is important — from now on, we crack down on publicity. We must give 'em the impression we don't want any more, that we're trying to hide something. That'll keep the boys going, even if Dobb fails us. By the way, Alan, is it true this niece of his has fallen for you in a big way?"

"No, it isn't," said Alan. "Lot of nonsense. There was a woman journalist — Helen Somebody — began talking that stuff to me. Don't encourage that rubbish. Mamber."

"I don't have to do a thing, if you ask me, from now on, my boys. By this time to-morrow the cuttings will be coming in sacks. And you did a very nice job with them, Lancelot. Many thanks."

"If necessary, I've always been able to handle the press. Usually I don't bother, of course, but if it should really be necessary—well, there I am." And Sir Lancelot cleared his throat importantly. "Hundreds of messages, I suppose, Mrs. Crisp? Naturally. Well, I'll talk to the Foreign Office, the British Council and the Arts Council—high-level people, of course, nobody else—and deal with the rest to-morrow—"

"Just a minute, Lancelot," said Alan, "before you float into the blue. I hate to spoil anything—and it's nice to see you and Mamber so pleased with each other—but I must tell you that you were talking rather wildly down in the drawing-room. To begin with, you've committed us to playing that symphony, Dobb or no Dobb, when Stannsen said we must have him. Yes, I know we've asked him, but so far we haven't got him. Next—you've just told the whole wide world that if necessary you're ready to use some other fantastic instrument, deeper than plummet ever sounded, and if there are any of these monsters, then—by crikey—we'll know it shortly. Wild words, Lancelot, wild, wild words—"

"Nonsense, my dear fellow. That's the sort of fighting speech they wanted to hear, and I leapt to the occasion, that's all. There's a jealous streak in you, my dear Alan, you'll have to watch. If some fellow turns up with a ridiculous instrument or two, what does it matter? We may even need him if the thing's any good. On the other hand, if Stannsen insists on this damned Dobbophone—and I must say it's about time he sobered up and talked sense—then pressure can be brought to bear on this idiotic fellow, Dobb, and he'll have to give in. The truth is, Alan, you're clean out of your depth, my boy." Sir Lancelot waved a hand, and tried to look like a Talleyrand in a check coat and yellow waistcoat. "This isn't just another concert. Official State visit, Government policy, international relations, national prestige, all that sort of thing comes into it. Which means that pressure can be brought to bear, quite apart from all this publicity stuff, and Dobb will have to behave himself."

"Absolutely," said Mamber. "And I'm beginning to wonder whose side you're on, Alan."

"For that matter so am I," said Alan. "All this pressure-to-bear talk! There's too much pressure about already. We're all having the juice squeezed out of us. So I say—*Up the Dobbs!*"

He marched out, bands playing, flags waving; and not merely

out of Lancelot's room but out of Radio Centre altogether. He made for the nearest post office, where he sent a telegram to Dobb: *Be prepared for appalling publicity and possible pressure to bear probably including fast dirty tricks. From a sincere well-wisher.* Then he spent one pound out of the windfall ten on cigars, went home, and worked until two in the morning.

He had to take a rehearsal of the Light Opera Orchestra next day, and it was after twelve when he paid his first visit to his office. Within five minutes, Miss Dobb was telephoning. "I do think you're mean," she announced. "This is the fifth time I've rung you up this morning and I've had to do it from call boxes. Why are they so smelly? Never mind, you can tell me afterwards. I have to ring you up because I promised Uncle Roland I wouldn't go near Radio Centre till he gave me permission. He's really furious, you know."

"I don't blame him. I won ten pounds yesterday because he wouldn't see Lancelot Telly and Mamber—"

"Then you can take me out to lunch. Somewhere very good. I'm terribly hungry."

"All right. Do you know *Chez Savarin?* Fabulously expensive— but very good. I'll meet you there at quarter to one."

He had to admit to himself that whatever Miss Dobb's faults might be, she was the right sort of girl to take to a restaurant, for instead of putting on airs and grumbling, as Mildred too often did, she was all smiles and eager anticipation, ready to enjoy everything. She looked uncommonly pretty too; all the chaps were taking her in, but she did not return their interested glances, he noticed with approval. He ordered a murderously expensive lunch.

"Are you truthful?" she asked, over the soles with grape sauce.

"Not specially."

"You must be or you wouldn't say that. Well, tell me the truth now. Did you send a telegram to my uncle calling yourself *A Sincere Well-wisher?*"

"Yes," said Alan.

"I knew it was you. Somehow I could tell at once. It's the only nice thing that's happened so far. Everything else has been beastly. Reporters and photographers hanging about all the time. Not that I mind, but Uncle does. Then messages from all kinds of mad people. It's in all the papers this morning, isn't it?"

"I gather from our publicity people it's in all the papers

everywhere—all over Western Europe. Probably in America, Asia and Africa too. By the end of the week your uncle will be a notorious world character."

"Mr. Fettle—that's Uncle's spivvy friend, you remember—wants to have a lot of tiny Dobbophones made. He says he could sell them like mad. But Uncle won't hear of it. And he's furious with me when he thinks I'm enjoying it. He's made me promise not to talk to anybody about him. Oh—what heavenly food!" They were now being served with cunningly seasoned mutton. "I wouldn't have thought you cared about food. You don't look greedy."

"I am—on and off," said Alan with the earnest pride of a man discussing his tastes. "I like to alternate between very good food and not bothering much, anything that's about. I hate indifferent stuff— cut off the joint and two veg—wet sweet muck in little glasses—that sort of thing. But tell me more about your uncle. I've taken a fancy to him."

"I thought you had. Why don't you take a fancy to me? All right, don't bother to reply. Well, I lost my father and mother in an aeroplane crash three years ago. Mother was a Norrolander— Stannsen was her second cousin—and that's how we all come to be mixed up with him. Then I spent two years with Uncle Roland in California, where they were using one of his inventions, something to do with radio for aircraft—and then I came back here with him. He's never been married—I think he was in love with somebody who died, but he never talks about it. He and Daddy were together in Norroland for a long time—so was I, though I came here to school— but though they were brothers they were quite different. Daddy was quiet and sensible whereas Uncle Roland's quite mad, though in a sweet sort of way, terribly kind really. But he's always getting angry about everything—"

"Quite right," said Alan. "So would I if I wasn't so busy with my music. Drink the claret with this mutton."

"Yes, but don't let me get tight. Either I laugh a lot at nothing or suddenly go to sleep—probably on your shoulder. You wouldn't like that, would you?"

"Not here—no."

"I wish you didn't look so dangerous and then turn out not to be, if you see what I mean. It's so confusing. However, about Uncle Roland. He never seems to believe what everybody else believes. And then gets furious about it. Most men—especially if they had inventions to sell—would be glad about all this publicity. But not Uncle Roland. He's dead against it—he's dead against nearly everything, yet he's not miserable and trying to spoil things—often he's enormous fun. Mr. Fettle, who's really a very tough sort of man behind all that wriggling, adores him. They're doing something together, probably to do with one of Uncle's inventions, but I don't know what it is. Probably illegal—because Uncle Roland doesn't care—and I'm sure Mr. Fettle's a rather nice kind of crook. He's smuggling Uncle out of the house to-day—in a wardrobe, I think." She started to laugh. "I suppose in a way Uncle Roland's enjoying it—if only because he really has something to be angry about now. But he won't give in, you know. Unless Stannsen apologises, or they play that silly game again, you'll never get him to bring his horrible Dobbophone to your concert. And what will you do then?"

"I don't know. Lancelot swears he'll perform the symphony. He's letting himself in for trying out other mad bass instruments—if they exist. And with all the fuss about it, we'll jolly well soon know. My guess is that nobody who's invented a lunatic bass monster will be able to resist all this publicity."

And indeed, as he was shortly to discover, he had guessed rightly. Already, Herr Julius Grobemeier of Mannheim had boarded the express for Cologne and the Hook of Holland, taking with him one of the wonders of the Rhineland—the Grobemeier *Great-German-Double-Bombardon,* six feet of shining brass and with a horn a yard in diameter. In Milan, one Nicola Bertini had taken apart and carefully packed his giant *contrafagotto,* half as big again as the ordinary bass bassoon, had borrowed *lire* from his three sisters, his four brothers, his father-in-law, and was about to buy a ticket for the night plane. And in a small villa on the outskirts of Clermont-Ferrand, those two inventive and ingenious musicians, Louis and Alfred Sauvager, middle-aged identical twins, small men and spare but with a piercing glance and long blue-black moustaches, were preparing for the journey to London, folding frilled dress shirts in tissue paper, and securely packing into its two cases their nine-foot two-man triple-bass fiddle, the terror of all *chefs d'orchestre* between Vichy and Avignon. At last, they told each other, they were within sight of *le grand soir,* when, before queens and presidents and milords, Louis would climb on to his little platform to handle the strings while Albert below sawed away with the two-handed bow, and the startled foggy air of London would vibrate to the glory of the Sauvager family, Clermont-Ferrand, and the department of Puy de Dome.

Meanwhile, lolling on the green-and-silver *banquettes* of *Chez Savarin,* lost in the fragrance of Havana smoke and coffee, Inga Dobb and Alan Applerose, like the Duke's followers in Arden, fleeted the time carelessly as they did in the golden world. . . .

CHAPTER IV

# SCHNAPPS

"FOR A young man of good family and background," said Sir Lancelot with some severity, "you seem to me to have had remarkably little social experience, Alan." They were on their way to the luncheon at the Norroland Embassy, but at this precise moment were sitting motionless in their taxi, immobile in an enormous traffic block in Piccadilly.

"Probably I was born twenty years too late—"

"My dear boy, good society still exists. The pretence that it doesn't comes from people who can't get into it."

"You'll have to polish that a bit, Lancelot. And don't waste this Gay Nineties stuff on me. You look as if you ought to be rattling towards this lunch in a hansom—"

"I wish I was, instead of sitting here, among all this hooting and carbon monoxide, watching these sixpences mount up. Always the same when I'm lunching anywhere—can't move. Where the devil do all these people come from?"

"I don't know where they come from," said Alan, "but they're all going to lunch on expense accounts. The trouble with my social ambitions," he continued dreamily, "is that they're at least sixty years out of date. I should like to have been the Lion of the Season— the explorer back from Darkest Africa, the young captain who did something on the North-West Frontier, the brilliant new novelist with the quizzical yet searching glance who's lured into the conservatory by Lady Kitty. As it is, whenever I reach the higher social levels nobody ever knows who I am and generally I talk at complete cross-purposes, so I begin to wonder if I'm tight. Sometimes I am."

"You have to show these people pretty plainly that you're a Personality," said Sir Lancelot, not without complacency. "I did it from the first. Assert yourself, my dear boy. If you want to talk about music, make 'em listen."

"I don't want to talk about music. However, I have hopes of this

Norroland Embassy. And Inga Dobb's going to be there, so I shall know somebody. You ought to put yourself right with that girl, Lancelot. Stannsen really is her godfather, and of course Roland Dobb's her uncle—"

Sir Lancelot frowned. "I'd like a short rest from that fellow. Good— we're moving again. By the way, there's a Policy Meeting this afternoon, with Dobb high on the agenda. You'd better come with me. We'll leave this lunch together. And don't overdo the Norroland schnapps."

Alan was just finishing his second glass, in an anteroom where there were about forty people, when Inga radiantly arrived from nowhere. "You're sitting next to me," she announced. "I've just fixed it with Erik Hafstalman. Do you like my new hair-do?"

"No."

"Why not?"

"I don't know. But then I've never liked any girl's new hair-do. They always look wrong somehow. But I've taken a great fancy to this Norroland schnapps. I wonder if there'll be time for another glass before we go in?"

"Lots. But you ought to eat something with it. Try the smoked salmon—it's marvellous. I'll get you some while you get some schnapps—just a drop for me too. There's loads of time. Norroland meals always have a lot of this preliminary eating and drinking."

While he was getting the schnapps, an elderly diplomatic type, not unlike a yellowish crocodile, greeted him in guttural French, asked after his wife, reminded him that they had last met in Belgrade, and then was removed by a very tall spectral woman with green spectacles, long before Alan could think of sufficient French to explain his identity. Inga returned with the smoked salmon and an outsize Viking who might have been Hafstalman's younger brother. He was not, it appeared, though Alan never caught his name. But he belonged to the same series, bellowing with laughter at any remark that contained the smallest grain of humour.

"He's rather in love with me," said Inga, after the giant had left them. "I'm rather fond of him too. He takes me to the ballet. Aren't you jealous?"

"Not in the least. A very nice fellow, though a bit too large and loud. You're right about this smoked salmon—much better than ours. Flown here, I suppose, along with cases of schnapps." He looked around. "Notice how these older diplomatic types look like overdone character parts in old-fashioned plays. Proves my point that all this foreign affairs business is out-of-date. How's your uncle?"

"He's having a terrific row now with the tax people. In fact, he told me this morning they may come and take all the furniture and things. If they do, I'm going to stay with the Hafstalmans."

"What will he do?"

"I think he'll stay with Joe Fettle—you know, the spivvy man. As it is, he spends most of his time at some mysterious place that Mr. Fettle runs. His Dobbophone thing is there already. He says you E.B.C. people might steal it. No I know *you* wouldn't, darling—you don't mind my calling you darling, do you?"

"Yes, I'm against it."

"But I wouldn't put anything past your Sir Lancelot. I can't bear him. Look at him over there—in those idiotic clothes—pretending to be so grand—"

"I don't need to look at him. I came here with him. Now what would you say," Alan continued, speaking with some care, "is the flavour of this schnapps? Not aniseed, I'd say. Perhaps—no—"

"It's a berry called *Dorsti* that you only find in Norroland. I'd also say," she added with smiling candour, "that you could easily be just a little bit tight already, my sweet pet. It's not what you say and do, which I think nothing of, but just your glowing dark eyes that make me call you my sweet pet. Look—we have to go in now. Come on."

On the other side of Alan, at the luncheon table, was a parchment-and-ivory old lady who was Baroness Somebody. Immediately she entangled him in the cross-purposes he had already mentioned to Sir Lancelot, for with no encouragement at all from him, she assumed at once that he was somebody she had known attached to the French Embassy, and without allowing him a word of protest, she talked at length about people and places he had never seen, occasionally nudging him sharply to emphasize a witty point. After trying a glass or two of wine, Alan had returned to schnapps, which appeared to him urgently necessary now that he had to cope with this mad Baroness. An occasional soft pressure on his left side reminded him that Inga was still there, pretending to listen to her neighbour, who seemed to be a midget minor diplomat, a blue-black satiny fellow probably from Latin America. The long table seemed longer than ever, with more people and odder people than there had been at first. Which of course was absurd, so absurd that Alan suddenly found himself laughing aloud. The Baroness nudged him in triumph. Three—or was it four?—blond giants across the table were holding up their glasses and looking at him in a fixed though smiling manner. Some sort of toast perhaps?

He drank to them. There came to him then an idea for an impudent piece, scored for small orchestra, to be called *Luncheon for Forty*— out of fashion among the new severities, no doubt, but not a bad idea. He drank to it.

As he might have guessed, the Norrolanders were great drinkers of official toasts, and now, with the last plates removed, they were at it, keeping him jumping up and down—Queen Elizabeth the Second— President of Norroland—Stannsen—even the English Broadcasting Company. Too many of the men now seemed to be either giants or midgets. An illusion possibly, but not without significance, that strange significance which appeared to be creeping into everything. He turned to Inga, with a question as to whether Norroland was famous for white or black magic, but the radiant face so close to his put the question out of his head. This was a very, very beautiful girl, and moreover a kind, sweet girl, ready to bring a man a plate of smoked salmon or one of her uncle's cigars. He told her so. Then, before she had time to stop him, he kissed her. It was no miserable peck at the cheek either, but a full long kiss on the lips.

It was as if he had pulled a string that wrecked the whole luncheon table. All the Norrolanders, male and female, jumped up and clapped and cheered. Then some of the women were kissing Inga, and he was being banged on the back by the giant Vikings. "What's happening?" he cried to Inga.

"We're engaged, darling. It's an old Norroland custom to announce an engagement like that. And you did it beautifully, darling."

"Did I? Oh—well—"

All the non-Norroland diplomatic types seemed to be delighted. Probably they had not seen a man get himself engaged for years, what with all those affairs with ballerinas and that sort of thing. The mad Baroness was nudging him with renewed zest. The only person there who looked displeased was Sir Lancelot, who was giving the betrothed pair a very sour look.

"Now they'll drink to our happiness," said Inga, who was having a wonderful time. "Then you have to drink the Betrothal Bumper— that's an old Norroland custom too. You're supposed to drink it without stopping, darling. Here it is."

Hafstalman handed him a glass goblet. "It is filled with the special old schnapps. Moch better, I think." And he roared with laughter. There were several short speeches in Norrolandish, punctuated by explosions of Viking mirth and some giggling from the blonde ladies; and to all of this, Inga, holding Alan's arm, listened in smiling composure, not even offering them the merest blush. The engaged pair were solemnly toasted. Then Inga replied briefly in Norrolandish, still without a blush or a tremor. "Now you say something, darling. And then you drink the Betrothal Bumper."

"After which I'll be out like a light," he muttered. He looked around, as steadily as he could. Inga squeezed his arm. The Baroness gave him a last nudge. "Well, ladies and gentlemen, thank you very much. I don't know much about Norroland—but I'm learning—and the more I learn the more I like you. This seems to me a very pleasant way of becoming engaged. And—er—thank you very much." He drained the goblet, felt the roof of his mouth go up in fire and smoke, saw with annoyance that somebody had set the room spinning like a top, closed his eyes and collapsed into a chair, pulling Inga, who was still clinging to his arm, down with him. The fiery darkness went round and round; there was distant laughter from the sagas; he was going to be sick and then sternly refused to be; and finally, after wandering among shadows, discovered that he was alone with Inga, who was persuading him to try some strong black coffee.

He stared about him. Yes, they were alone. "I never had a cigar either," he announced.

Inga laughed. "Darling, you're still tight. No, it's all right—you were wonderful. It was Erik Hafstalman's fault, giving you the very strong old schnapps. How do you feel now?"

"Peculiar." He sat up properly. "Everything's very clear—but not sensible. Did Lancelot go?"

"Yes. He was furious. Do you love me?"

"Certainly," he replied promptly, to his own surprise. "Come here, girl." He took her in his arms and kissed her with tremendous passion and skill, surprising himself again.

"I adore you," she said.

"And so you ought." He would have kissed her again, at even greater length and strength, only at that moment Hafstalman came in, with a Brunhilde who was Mrs. Hafstalman.

"I am so very happy for you," cried Mrs. Hafstalman. "And tonight you are coming with dear Inga to our house for a little betrothal dinner."

"Am I? Splendid! Thank you very much, Mrs. Hafstalman—and Mr. Hafstalman—and of course Miss Dobb—"

"Darling, aren't you still a little—"

"Certainly not," he told her sharply. "On the contrary. Calm and clear. Ready for anything, including a Policy Meeting of the E.B.C. which I must now hurry off to attend." He looked at them sternly. "For the honour of Norroland. For the sake of Stannsen. And Dobb. There might be dirty work being plotted. I'll put a stop to it."

Hafstalman roared with laughter, ignoring the reproachful glances of his wife and Inga. "You are now in what we call the *Schnapps-sunlight*—it is not dronk—but somethings else—"

"I don't believe it *is* anything else," said Inga.

"No, no—he's quite right. Calm and clear—that's the watchword." He shook hands with the Hafstalmans and kissed Inga. "Never did I see the path of duty so clearly. And we meet, as you say, to-night. But not, I think, Mr. Hafstalman—the special old schnapps."

"Inga and I will speak of the wedding," cried Mrs. Hafstalman.

Alan waved a hand. "Make any arrangements you please, ladies. Applerose is your man. I must make all speed to Radio Centre."

"I can send you in a car," said Hafstalman.

"An excellent idea. Thank you."

Calm and clear, he climbed into the Embassy car, lit the fine cigar that had somehow found its way into his pocket, and allowed himself to be conveyed majestically through the sullen afternoon to Radio Centre. Still calm and clear, but with the cigar poised at a rakish and almost sinister angle, he summoned the lift to take him straight up to the meeting, not even troubling to look into his own room, marched in and took the best place he could find. "Sorry I'm late," he announced, in a magnificently calm, clear tone.

Sir Lancelot looked at him with distaste that was heightened by alarm. "No, no, Applerose. I shan't want you here after all."

"Nonsense!" Alan waved his cigar. "I must be here. Questions of principle may be involved." He looked round sternly. "Carry on, Mr. Chairman."

The Air Marshal stared at him. He stared back, replacing the cigar in the corner of his mouth, and then leaning back and folding his arms.

"Well," said the Air Marshal rather sourly, "we're discussing this

Dobb business, so I suppose you might have something to say. Yes, Porton?"

"With all due respect, sir," said Porton, "my own view is that in the circumstances we'd be justified in bringing some pressure to bear on this man Dobb. It's a risk, of course. But if anything came out, we could count on the support of most of the popular press and public opinion. After all, here's an occasion of national importance—"

"Yes, yes, we all understand that," said the Air Marshal. "And we're all agreed the man's behaving stupidly, probably to attract attention to himself—"

"Certainly not," cried Alan. "I can't accept that. I've met Dobb— and you haven't—and I can assure you he's no desire to attract attention to himself. He detests publicity, as we ought to know by this time. He's—"

"All right, Applerose, you've made your point." The Air Marshal looked dubiously at Porton. "All very well talking about bringing pressure to bear, but easier said than done. What have you in mind?"

Porton wriggled. "I'd prefer not to answer that question, sir, with all due respect. Especially as Applerose seems to extend more sympathy to Dobb than he does to us. But perhaps Mamber and I—"

"I'm ready to suggest a few ideas," said Mamber. "And I hear that Dobb's having trouble with the tax people. We can dream up something to make him change his mind."

"But you can't guarantee to bring it off," said the Air Marshal. There were murmurs of agreement from several people. "And time's getting on. What do you say, Telly? It's really your pigeon."

"I have announced," Sir Lancelot began, in his haughtiest tone, "that I shall perform Stannsen's symphony at this special concert, and I propose to keep my word. I shall perform it with or without Dobb."

"You can't perform it without Dobb," said Alan.

Sir Lancelot ignored him. "For my part I propose to forget about Dobb and his nonsensical instrument. And I think it would be a mistake now to give this business any further publicity. I have followed the composer's suggestion and have asked Dobb to play his instrument. If at the last moment Stannsen discovers that Dobb is not playing, he cannot possibly cancel the performance, not with a concert of this kind, on the highest possible level. I suggest therefore, Mr. Chairman, that we make no further approaches to Dobb, allowing him to return to the obscurity he apparently enjoys, publicize the concert without any reference to him, and in short forget about the fellow."

Westfort and several of the others immediately showed their approval of this policy. The Air Marshal seemed to be in favour of it too, even after Mamber had pointed out that the popular press might be still interested in Dobb and that it was a pity to try and kill such a whale of a story. Obviously it was time for a man who was calm and clear, yet vowed to the pursuit of truth and justice, to speak his mind. Alan took out his cigar and rapped sharply on the table.

"Mr. Chairman, I disagree," he began, feeling at once masterful and happy. "I refuse to accept such a contemptible policy."

"Possibly," said the Air Marshal dryly. "But I don't remember asking you for your opinion, Applerose."

"But as Assistant Director of Music I consider I have a right to express my opinion." As the Air Marshal and Sir Lancelot tried to say something, Alan stood up and thumped the table, all in a calm and clear fashion. "Stannsen told us definitely—*No Dobbophone, no symphony.* Probably the only reason why he offered us the first performance of this work is because he knew Dobb was here in London. He knows very well that there are many better symphony orchestras at his disposal than ours, which would be a lot better if so many of the players were not always being taken away to perform all sorts of rubbish. If we can't guarantee Dobb and his Dobbophone, then we're deliberately deceiving a great man—a man of genius—a man who makes people like us look like mad mice." There were cries of protest, but he shouted them down. "You spend your time trying to please a lot of nitwits who haven't the sense to amuse themselves for an hour or two every night, who want to pay tuppence a week and have every idiotic prejudice considered and catered for, who can't even play their own parlour games any more. Yet when a man of genius offers us a work of genius, we begin plotting how to deceive him, shuffling and lying—"

The purple Air Marshal, now on his feet too, found his parade ground voice. "Drop this nonsense, Applerose. Clear out."

"Certainly. But please note I refuse to be a party to—"

"And another thing," roared the Air Marshal. "As you seem to dislike this organization, I suggest you resign from it as soon as possible—"

"Mr. Chairman, he's been lunching," cried Sir Lancelot. "Special circumstances—I'll explain later—"

"Don't bother, Lancelot," said Alan. He looked at the Air Marshal, who had now sat down again. "You want my resignation, Mr. Chairman? Consider you've got it. Good afternoon." And he stalked out, still calm and clear.

He seemed to hear some strange sounds along the corridor belonging to the Music Department, but he ignored them and went into his room, to compose a magnificent letter of resignation. Before he could decide whether to adopt a lofty tone or one of bitter irony, Mrs. Crisp came fluttering in, not at all her usual large Corn Queen self. "Oh—Alan—have you been up at the Meeting?"

"I have, Mrs. Crisp. In fact, I've just told the Meeting what I think of it. For the first and last time."

"Oh—Alan—what's the matter with you? You're not tight, are you?"

"Tight? Certainly not. What an idea! Do I look tight? Do I sound tight?"

"Not exactly, dear, no. But there seems to be *something* —"

"Have you ever heard of *Schnapps-sunlight*, Mrs. Crisp? No, I thought not. Well, imagine an afternoon in early spring not far from the Arctic Circle the cool, clear light—"

"Alan, do please stop. You can tell me some other time. I must know about Sir Lancelot. Will he be down soon?"

"I couldn't tell you," said Alan loftily. "No doubt plots are being hatched up there that may keep him for another hour or so. Why?"

Mrs. Crisp looked as if she did not know whether to laugh or cry. "Because I can't stand it much longer. The British Council have sent four foreigners to see him—and they're waiting in his room."

"No harm in that. I've no doubt Lancelot will be delighted to meet four foreigners, even if they have been sent by the British Council—"

"No, Alan, you don't understand. They've brought these awful instruments—and they keep wanting to try them. And you never saw or heard such things."

Above his continuing calmness and clarity there rose, like the sun of schnapps, a terrible joy. It brought Alan from his desk to clasp Mrs. Crisp's fat arms. "Would these be very large and very deep bass instruments? They would? Then leave these gentlemen to me, dear Mrs. Crisp. Your troubles are over. I'll take charge of them—"

"Oh—Alan—I wish you would—"

"I will. And you might thank the British Council for delivering them all in one package to us. Not in my name, of course—as from Sir Lancelot. By the way, talking of names—have you got theirs? You have? Yes? Herr Julius Grobemeier, of Mannheim. Yes? Signor Nicola Bertini, of Milan. Good! Messieurs Louis and Alfred Sauvager, of Clermont-Ferrand. Not brothers, are they? Twins? Ah—wonderful are the works of destiny! Now, Mrs. Crisp, there's nothing more for you to do except to thank the British Council. I'll take charge. It's the very least I can do."

"I must say, Alan dear," cried Mrs. Crisp, looking as if she wanted to kiss him, "you're very sweet and helpful always. I don't know what we'd do without you. It isn't true, is it, that you've just got engaged? I thought it was just some of Sir Lancelot's nonsense."

"No, it's some of my nonsense. I'm engaged in the old Norroland fashion, in full *Schnapps-sunlight*. I've also resigned from the E.B.C."

"No, Alan, I don't believe it. You *are* tight, you know, in a funny sort of way—"

"Mrs. Crisp, there's work to be done." He patted her shoulder and went floating past her, into Lancelot's room. And there they were, all eager, expectant, and supporting instruments out of a conductor's nightmare.

"Herr Grobemeier?" he cried.

The fattest of them bowed, beamed, held out an enormous hand.

"A great honour," said Alan gravely, shaking the hand. "And what have you brought us? The *Great-German-Double-Bombardon?* I've heard of it, of course. Who hasn't? Signor Nicola Bertini?"

"Si, si, signor." This was the thin, sad man who was holding the gigantic contra-bassoon, a shining black monster. "Ees vera beega *contra-fagotto*. Okay. I play heem fora you, pliz?"

"Not now," said Alan hastily. *"Piu presto possibile—decimo minuti."* He now turned to the Frenchmen and, calm and clear though he was, he nearly gave a yell at the sight of them and their monstrous instrument. They were exactly alike, little men with the same black glassy eyes and unreal moustaches, but one stood to attention with the massive bow clasped in both hands while the other had mounted to a little platform, ready to manipulate the rope-like strings. "Messieurs Louis *et* Alfred Sauvager?" They bowed together. This gave Alan time to take hold of himself. *"Wunderschon—*I mean, *magnifique!* Your own invention? It must be. *Non, non—ne jouez* *pas maintenant, je vous prie, messieurs. Pas ici. En haut—dans un moment—pour les grands directeurs de E.B.C."* Taking further hold of himself, and dismissing the notion that all these were apparitions of *Schnapps-sunlight,* he looked round at the four of them, put on a solemn official look, and, with the help of all the scraps of German, Italian, French, he could remember, made them understand that Sir Lancelot was attending a grand conference of E.B.C. directors, and that it was his privilege and pleasure to escort them to the conference room, where they would be able at once to demonstrate the range and sonority of their ingenious instruments. So all they had to do was to follow him. *Vorwärts! Avanti! En avant!*

Calm and clear in exquisite *Schnapps-sunlight,* floating along as in a dream, he led them onward and upward, tossing various scraps of foreign languages over his shoulder, giving them courage and confidence as they panted beneath the bulk and weight of their fabulous instruments. When he stopped outside the door of the conference room, he saw that the procession had collected a number of grinning followers, engineers and effects boys and the like. He regarded them sternly and waved them back. Then he listened for a moment: the Policy Meeting had not finished; Westfort was spinning one of his metaphysical-cum-psychological chicaneries. Just the right moment. After a brief message of good-will, he threw open the door and hastily guided the monsters in. Above the cries of protest, he heard, as he closed the door, the first fearful blast of the *Great-German-Double-Bombardon,* which seemed to be followed at once by the death rattle of a brontosaurus, no doubt the giant *contra-fagotto* trying out one of its higher notes; and then, though he did not stay to listen, he knew that pandemonium had broken loose. He moved delicately down the corridor, lightly brushing his hands together.

"Here, listen to that!" cried one of the engineers. "What's on, Mr. Applerose?"

"We're trying out a few new bass instruments. Must move with the times, you know. Progress—progress! Go along and listen properly."

Back in his room, he hastily began assembling all the things he wanted to take home. Mrs. Crisp came in. "Mildred Povey's just been in. She was livid. She never wants to speak to you again. She's left you a note." Alan waved away any consideration of Mildred's note. "As you know, I'm engaged elsewhere—in the old true Norroland fashion—"

"What have you done with those foreigners?"

"I've let them loose into the Policy Meeting—"

"Oh—my goodness!"

"Nobody, my dear Mrs. Crisp," said Alan gravely, "appreciates your goodness more than I do. I shall miss it." He gave her a hug and a hearty kiss. "Tell Mildred from me to look for a better man. She'll easily find one, though not on the Fourth Programme, where they've hardly seen any kind of man for years. Give Lancelot my regards— and tell him to stop over-dramatizing and pansying up his Brahms. I think that's all—"

"Oh—Alan—I *know* you're tight. *Do* go home."

"I'm going—for good. I've gone. Good-bye, Mrs. Crisp."

On his way home it seemed to him that an uneasy dusk was creeping into the *Schnapps-sunlight*. The calmness and the clearness were going. And no sooner had he tried to quench his mounting thirst with several glasses of water, tasting queerly of schnapps, than the Arctic night began to close over his mind. He stretched himself out on his wide old sofa, with some vague notion of taking stock of the day's events, and immediately fell asleep. It was after midnight when he awoke, stiff and cold and with a head that somebody seemed to be sawing in half. Slowly, with much caution, he began to work things out. Undoubtedly he had attended a luncheon at the Norroland Embassy. So much was certain. But after that all was shadowy, not to be distinguished from dream stuff. He bathed his head, brewed some tea, and stared with aching eyes at a miniature score of the Mozart quintet for violin, two violas, horn and 'cello. But he could not escape the feeling that a good deal had happened during the afternoon. The girl, Inga Dobb, came into it, and schnapps, and Sir Lancelot and the Air Marshal; and at one moment he imagined he had actually met four foreigners with fantastic instruments and had marched them into a Policy Meeting. Then he laughed at himself. It served him right for sleeping and dreaming when he ought to have been hard at work. But it was queer, he thought as he concentrated on Mozart's handling of the second viola, how this dream nonsense lingered in a fellow's mind.

# CHAPTER V

# NOVELTIES

AT NOON next day Alan was at the Norroland Embassy again, this time in Hafstalman's room, pleasantly furnished in the clean, light Scandinavian fashion. But Alan, still suffering from his hangover, regarded it without pleasure. A fierce telegram from Inga, waiting for him at Radio Centre, had compelled him to pay this visit.

"It was not your fault of course," Hafstalman was saying. "You were soffering from what we call *Schnapps-sunlight.*" And he roared with laughter, making Alan wince.

"So that's what you call it," said Alan. "I knew I couldn't have invented that. I suddenly remembered it, last night. Well then, you see how it was, Mr. Hafstalman. When I got home, I went to sleep, forgetting I had a dinner engagement with you and Mrs. Hafstalman. I'm terribly sorry. I may say that's nothing to what I did at the E.B.C."

"Of this I have already heard some things," said Hafstalman, looking serious now. "There is a Norroland girl works in Radio Centre who tells me useful things, so she rang me this morning to tell me what she had heard. She tells me you were friendly to Stannsen and Norroland interests. That is fine. But does this mean you have lost your yob?"

"My yob?" Alan was startled. What had he done now?

"Your position with E.B.C."

"Oh—yes, I've lost that. I dare say they'd have me back—because Telly knows how useful I am—if I'd go round and apologize to everybody, but I don't feel like doing that. I'm tired of them, anyhow. The money was useful, but I'll manage somehow. But tell me, Mr. Hafstalman, why am I supposed to be here? More apologies?"

"It is the women, you understand." Hafstalman hesitated, probably wondering if a Viking gale of laughter would help and then deciding against it. "It is the same thing always with the women—they know when a man is dronk, when sober—but not about *Schnapps-sunlight,* which they have never themselves. So they are angry because you do not come to the dinner. They do not understand that you forget. And Inga does not know your address, and when she has to say this, then she is more angry, and then my wife is more angry for her."

"Quite right," said Alan. "It must be humiliating to be engaged to a man if you don't know where he lives. But of course I'd have given her my address if I'd known we were about to become engaged. The trouble is, I didn't know."

Hafstalman made an enormous clucking sound of sympathy. "Inga is a nice girl, very pretty. I ask a personal question, Mr. Applerose. You are in lof with Inga?"

"I didn't know I was, but from what you've told me I must have been towards the end of lunch yesterday. Of course I'd had a lot of schnapps. That may mean that when my inhibitions are removed I find I am in love with her. On the other hand, it may mean that if I drink enough schnapps I begin to fancy any pretty wench who's sitting next to me. So the only honest answer I can give you is—I don't know. But what happens this morning?"

"It is another old Norroland custom," said Hafstalman gravely. "Inga likes our old Norroland customs, I think, perhaps because they remind her of her dear mother, who was Norrolander, you know. It is the old Betrothal Breaking ceremony, you must understand."

"I see," said Alan dubiously. "What—er—happens?"

"It is very simple. There must be three witnesses. My wife will come with Inga—and I will ask one of my colleagues to come as witness too." He looked at his watch. "It is time now. You would like a drink perhaps before the ceremony—schnapps?"

"I could do with one, on the hair of the dog principle. But I'd better not, thanks. The women might be angrier still if they think I'm still tippling. Perhaps a spot after the—er—ceremony, if that's allowed."

"It is part of the ceremony," said Hafstalman smiling. "You drink the Breaking Bumper—special old schnapps—"

Alan stared at him doubtfully. "I seem to have heard that before. However—"

He said no more because at that moment Inga and Mrs. Hafstalman came in, looking as if they had come to examine, on behalf of the public health authorities, a nest of plague-stricken rats.

Even Hafstalman began to look guilty.

"Mrs. Hafstalman," cried Alan desperately, "I do most humbly apologize for not remembering your kind invitation last night. You see—"

"It is nothing," said Mrs. Hafstalman, with an air of cold finality.

"*Schnapps-sunlight*," muttered Hafstalman. The women gave him one glance and then closed their eyes. Alan looked appealingly at Inga, who opened her eyes to stare right through him. He would have said something to her but Hafstalman's colleague, the third witness, now arrived. He was shorter than Hafstalman but immensely broad, and seemed to have one sympathetic eye, for Alan and Hafstalman, and one cold and contemptuous eye, which agreed with the ladies. He was introduced to Alan as Dr. Trock. This remarkable difference between his eyes only added to Alan's bewilderment. It was hard to believe Dr. Trock was quite real. Then, before anybody could say anything, an elderly woman servant in black, probably Peer Gynt's mother, entered carrying a tray of glasses and schnapps.

Hafstalman said something in Norrolandish to Inga, who replied in Norrolandish, obviously repeating some formula. Both Hafstalmans and Dr. Trock said something in Norrolandish. Alan began to feel like some timid minor character in a saga. There was a pause. What happened next? He soon knew.

Inga stepped forward briskly, and, without warning, gave him a fearful clout, easily the worst he had had since he was ten. "Here— what the—" he cried as he reeled.

The English half of her took charge now. "And serve you jolly well right, Alan Applerose. Now we're not engaged."

"Now we drink," said Hafstalman soothingly to the outraged Alan. "Then you drink the Breaking Bumper. And that is the Betrothal Breaking ceremony."

As he watched them lift their glasses, the men with enthusiasm, the women formally and with some distaste, Alan felt like shattering Miss Inga's complacency with a good belt across the lug. But he restrained himself and at a signal from Hafstalman he gloomily picked up the hefty goblet assigned to him, which must have held about a quarter of a pint of schnapps.

"In Norroland," said Dr. Trock, "it is tradition to trink him in one swallow."

They all stared at Alan, Inga with rather more interest than she had displayed before. "Well, here goes," he cried. "This is the first time I've been engaged, and I hope it's the last. Here's to freedom!" Down it went, and at once there was something familiar about the queer sensations that followed its progress, swift and fiery as a torchlight procession of jet aircraft. As he came out of the smoke and flames, he glared at Inga, undoubtedly a most beautiful and desirable girl but one who would be none the worse for a good hiding. "What about your uncle?" he demanded sharply, still glaring at her.

"I've quarrelled with him just as I have with you," she replied, with equal sharpness.

"Then you ought to be ashamed of yourself. I'm going straight to him. His to command. Roland Dobb—the Man of the Hour. The great No man. I've half a mind to return that bang on the ear you gave me," he added, glowering.

"You touch me! You daren't—"

He grabbed hold of her, gave her a smacking kiss, then a little slap on the cheek. "That's an old English custom," he said hurriedly. "Known as the Good-bye-to-the-cheeky-girl Ceremony. Thanks for the drink, Hafstalman. Good-bye. Good-bye." And he left with such haste that he forgot the only hat he possessed.

It was raining. All the taxis were engaged, the buses full. The fire of the schnapps perished under the sodden weight of London. It took him half an hour to reach the pub near Radio Centre where he usually had a drink and a sandwich with his musical colleagues of the E.B.C. The place was crowded, but not a single instrumentalist of his acquaintance was there; probably the symphony orchestra was still rehearsing. The people who were there seemed lumpy, wettish, and dull; the drinks were too warm, the food too cold; and the newspaper he picked up brought no comfort. There were times when Alan enjoyed London, but this was not one of them. He set out in a melancholy drizzle for Marlin Gardens, Hampstead, praying that he would find Dobb there.

There was a large van outside Dobb's house; several gloomy men were loading it with furniture. The hall looked very forlorn. The rooms he passed on his way up to the second floor seemed to have been already cleared. Dobb was sitting in his workroom, looking at some notes and eating a leg of cold roast chicken. This time he was wearing what appeared to be a fisherman's jersey and crimson corduroy trousers. He did not look up when Alan walked in.

"Oh—Mr. Dobb—"

"Go away," said Dobb. But then he looked up. "Oh—it's you, Applejohn."

"Let's get this settled, once and for all, Mr. Dobb," said Alan firmly. "I'm Applerose—*rose* and not Applejohn."

"Quite right. Well now, Applerose, what about you? Let's get that settled too. If you've come again on behalf of that radio gang, you're wasting your time."

"I haven't. As a matter of fact, I've had a row with them, chiefly on your behalf, and now I'm out."

"Sit down, then. There's some more cold chicken in a paper bag over there, but I can't recommend it. Don't want to eat? Neither do I—not this stuff. Have a cigar? You're the chap who likes cigars, aren't you?"

"I am," said Alan with enthusiasm. They lit two magnificent Havanas; he felt better at once.

"Well now," said Dobb, "what about you and my niece, Inga? She talks such nonsense that I don't listen to half she says, though I'm devoted to the child. What's going on between you?"

Alan explained as best he could how he had become involved in the old Norroland betrothal ceremony, then described in much greater detail the Breaking ceremony. "I asked about you," he went on, "and she told me she'd quarrelled with you just as she had with me. So I said that I was coming straight to you. By the way, are you moving from here?"

"They're taking my furniture and effects to pay these taxes they say I owe them," said Dobb carelessly. "I don't seem very popular at the moment, what with one thing and another."

"You're very popular with me, Mr. Dobb. I don't suppose there's anything I can do for you, but if there is, I'll do it. I haven't much of a place—two rooms and a third share of a bath—but if you'd like a bed—"

"No, thanks, Applerose. Very good of you, but all that's taken care of. I've arranged to stay with a friend of mine called Joe Fettle—"

"I met him here. A rather wriggly cockney type—"

"That's Joe. Well, he's a good friend of mine, so he's putting me up." He stared at Alan speculatively, then grinned, his heavy lined face lighting up in the most wonderful fashion, his eyes glittering with mischief. "Applerose, if you mean what you say—and most people don't seem to do, nowadays—you could do something for me. But it might get you into trouble. How do you feel about that?"

"I seem to be in trouble now. I might as well be in some more. And anyhow," Alan added, "I was getting into a rut. It's what happens in Radio Centre. If you're not one of the active intriguers, which I never was, you soon begin to feel you must be sleep-walking. What do I do, Mr. Dobb?"

"Just Dobb, please, Applerose. This is the position. I've invented—"

But there he stopped short because two of the removal men came into the room, and without a word picked up two chairs and a table and took them away. Alan now noticed that all the note-books, blue-prints, little gadgets, maps, plans, photographs, which he had remarked before, had already gone. He looked enquiringly at Dobb.

"Yes, all my more important stuff, connected with my work, I took across to Fettle's place yesterday. He has a car—several, in fact—and I haven't and I'm waiting for him to call for me. If he's agreeable, I'd better take you along. I don't like saying too much with these fellows around."

The two men returned, followed by a third, and between them, all in silence, they cleared away the rest of the tables.

"If these were my possessions," said Alan, "I'd be making more fuss than you seem to be doing. Bit much, isn't it—just carting everything away like this? What do they do? Sell it by auction?"

"Apparently," said Dobb with a careless wave of the hand. "But I've arranged with Joe Fettle to buy all the things I want to keep. At a reasonable figure, of course."

"But what if the auctioneer runs them up to unreasonable figures?"

"Joe's attending to that. He understands about these things. He's a rascal, of course, Joe is, a thoroughly bad citizen, but I'm very fond of him and for some reason or other he's rather devoted to me. Do your best to get along with him, Applerose. Otherwise, you wouldn't be much use to me. He's rather sensitive and punctilious, outside business; like most newly self-made men, anxious to climb socially."

"What *is* his business?" Alan demanded bluntly. "Some sort of spivvery?"

"That's what I mean, Applerose. You can talk to me like that, but don't try it with Joe. You might say he's a sort of general dealer in a rather loose but very enterprising fashion. Don't make a mistake about him." Dobb lowered his voice. "Most of his business must be illegal—having been made illegal by preposterous legislation—but he wouldn't touch stolen goods or anything of that sort. In his own way, he's honest enough, and very much a man of his word, which is more than most politicians could truthfully say of themselves; but, like me, he's against the government. However, I've nothing to do with his business enterprises, don't know what most of 'em are. We met in a pub—I liked him, he liked me—and we've worked out a little scheme together—"

This time the three men wanted the two chairs that Alan and Dobb were sitting in, and waited, still without a word, for them to get up. "What about them cigar boxes?" asked one of the men.

"Over my dead body," said Alan, horrified.

"That's the spirit, Applerose," said Dobb. "These cigar boxes are opened and in use, and you fellows can't touch them. Now off you go, and leave us alone."

The oldest of the men lingered. "We've left everything as tidy as we could, Mr. Dobb."

Dobb held his hand out, as if to receive the tip that the man clearly expected. "What about giving me a tip for providing you with a good day's work? No? Then we won't have any tipping—humph? Good afternoon."

"Since when?" said the man, and heavily departed.

"Don't think I'm mean, Applerose. I hope I'm not. But these fellows should decide which world they want to live in—the old world of tips, or the new world of guaranteed wages, short hours, and everything laid on. Don't see why they should have both."

"Don't see why you should tip a man when you haven't asked him to take away your furniture. What about these cigar boxes? Are we taking them with us?"

They carried four each and went down to the ground floor. The men had gone. The house looked very forlorn indeed now; the afternoon was darkening and still drizzling; Alan, though still enjoying his cigar, felt melancholy. He confessed as much to Dobb.

"A great mistake," said Dobb briskly. "The trick is—never open yourself to the influence of the environment unless it's unusually favourable. Just ignore your surroundings. Probably more difficult for you, because you're a kind of artist. But try it. I've had to learn to do it because I've been stuck in some hellish places in my time.

Not sure this London of today isn't one of 'em. Don't care for it any more. Lost its old character, rather sinister in its extremes of wealth and poverty but very romantic, and hasn't acquired a new one worth having. Or if it has, I don't see it. This sounds like Joe Fettle."

It was. He was driving one of those very wide American cars that look like angry giant toads. Fortunately, when he joined them in the hall, he remembered meeting Alan before; indeed, he seemed to know more about him than Dobb had done. "Miss Inga's Boy Friend. She's told me one or two things. I told the wife, an' she was on it right off. Knew your name from the E.B.C., she did, Mr. Applerose. Because why? Barmy on music, the wife is. You come an' tickle the ivories for her—we got a lovely instrument, proper big grand, wouldn't have no less, she wouldn't—an' she'll be out of her mind. Listen by the hour, not sayin' a word. Marvellous! Very pleased to meet again, Mr. Applerose, very pleased."

"A great pleasure, Mr. Fettle," said Alan, remembering Dobb's instructions.

"Thankin' you," said Fettle. "Well, Mr. Dobb, what's cookin'?"

"We've agreed we ought to have somebody with radio programme experience," said Dobb. "I think Applerose is the man, if he's game. He's left the E.B.C., after telling 'em what he thought of their monkey tricks with me. So he's all right—one of us. So now I'll put it to him, if you're agreeable."

"Honoured I'm sure," said Fettle, with an ultra-polite wriggle. Nevertheless, he gave Alan a very shrewd and searching look. What he saw seemed to satisfy him. "The wife'll be pleased too. Spill it, Mr. Dobb."

"I've done a lot of radio work in my time," said Dobb. "Now I've invented a new type of transmitter—small, compact, very powerful within a short radius. Know anything about the technical side of radio?"

"Not a thing," Alan told him hurriedly.

"Same here," said Fettle. "It's conjurin' to me. Might as well do it with mirrors. Sorry, Mr. Dobb. Won't interrupt."

"I've rigged it up on the top floor of Joe's warehouse," Dobb went on. "And it's about ready now to be tried out. That's why I want some help. Now I can't say any more unless you're ready to come in with us. It's illegal, of course. We may be dodging the police soon. Only fair to warn you."

"I'm in," said Alan. "I'm not sure what I can do to help, but I'll try to do it."

"We shake on it," cried Fettle. And they solemnly shook hands. "Better be off, Mr. Dobb. I was late gettin' here."

There was ample room for the three of them on the front seat of the American car. "My idea," said Dobb as they moved off, "is to run my own radio programme for a week or two. But before that I'll cut into the E.B.C. programmes for a few nights. I can do it in the London area with this transmitter of mine. Waken people up. Do 'em good."

"Certainly," said Alan. "But won't the E.B.C. engineers soon find out where you're transmitting from?"

"Sooner or later they will. But I've a little device that will hold 'em up for a week or two, even if they go all out to stop me. What I want you to do, Applerose, is to organize some music for my programme. Must have some good music. That and a few home truths are the only things worth listening to in radio. You'll have to record the music—can't run a studio, of course, in these circumstances; but I've a beautiful little recording machine, my own invention, I can let you have. Chamber music, naturally. We can't run to hiring orchestras."

"You'd soon have trouble with the Musicians' Union if you did," said Alan. "I can find you some good rebels for chamber music." He hesitated. "The trouble is—we ought to pay 'em *something*. That's only fair. I'm ready to do what I can. But I haven't much to spare, and I'll soon have less, now that I'm out of the E.B.C.—"

"No, no, no. We'll pay 'em," cried Dobb. "Pay 'em well too. I was ready to do that myself, but Joe here has a scheme. No, don't try to explain now, Joe. Keep your mind on your driving."

"Whatever you say, Mr. Dobb. But I could drive this bus in my sleep. Just tryin' it out. Got it as part of a nice little deal last Tuesday—I'm sellin' it next week. Thirteen hundred cash—or I'm a monkey. Don't touch cheques. All a cash trade, mine is."

They finally came to a halt in a short street somewhere in the region between King's Cross station and Islington. The warehouse was boldly labelled Union Jack Novelty Co. "An' don't kid yourself, Mr. Applerose," said Fettle as he took them in, "we got plenty of novelties here. Doin' a nice trade—all legit—for Christmas. Everything for the kiddies. Lovely lines, we have. How's it goin', Bert? Good! I'm upstairs if I'm wanted, but only if it's urgent." He took them past crates of novelties to a goods hoist, which stopped at the second floor. On one side, open to view, was another room filled with novelties, but when Alan made a move to get out that way, he was stopped by Dobb, who indicated the other side, apparently a solid wall. To Alan's astonishment and then immediate delight, Fettle put a hand to the wall and it swung open. "Clever, eh? My idea but of course I got a nexpert to work out the doin's. After you, if you please, Mr. Applerose, Mr. Dobb."

They were now in a large room equally crowded with goods, which might also be called novelties—for many people had not seen very much of them for a long time. There seemed to be cases of whisky and other liquors, among other things that Alan had no time to notice in detail. Cigars too, he fancied hopefully. But they were moving towards a spiral iron stairway.

"Don't get me wrong, Mr. Applerose," said Fettle earnestly. "I'm no fence. None of the lorry boys bring anything here. Wouldn't touch the stuff. All honest tradin', this lot. What *I* call honest, anyhow. Board of Trade an' Inland Revenue might think diff'rent, but we can't let these chaps in striped pants have it all their own way, can we, Mr. Applerose? Enterprise must go on."

They climbed this stairway, then another, which offered an equally enticing view of rich novelties, and arrived at the fourth floor. Here the room was much smaller, contained no crates, cases and bales, and clearly belonged to Dobb rather than to Fettle. Most of it, in fact, was filled with apparatus that was apparently being worshipped by an oldish and rather melancholy man in overalls.

"This is the transmitter," said Dobb. "And this is Ted, who's been helping me. Applerose, put those cigar boxes on the shelf there. I'll take mine round to Joe's place. Now, Ted, what do you think?" And the two of them were immediately lost in technicalities and began doing something to the apparatus.

"Between you an' I, Mr. Applerose," Fettle whispered, taking Alan away from the other two, "you can get straight from here to my place, but I'm not goin' to show you how while Ted's about. I'm not sayin' Ted's not all right, but you can't have too many in the know, can you? So when Mr. Dobb's finished here, we'll go down again, an' go round to my place that way. Got a lovely home, though you wouldn't think so from the outside. The wife wants to move, of course—service flat in the West End, all posh—but this is a lot handier for me."

"I can imagine that, Mr. Fettle. You must have quite a large enterprise here, what with—er—one thing and another. If you don't mind my asking, how did you manage to start such a business?"

It was obvious that Fettle was much gratified. "Anything you ask, Mr. Applerose, I'll tell you. I'm in the Navy in the war, see—volunteer, though I'm gettin' on for forty. All right. I come out, war over. Got a few bobs—an' the wife has some too through her old man —so I start a little business, something I know about, something that's wanted—furnishin's and accessories for caffs—chiefly North-East London trade. Mr. Applerose, it's bloody murder from the word Go. They're on top of me right from the start. I can't do this, I can't do that. I can't have this, I can't have that. You'd think I was runnin' a knockin' shop, the way these officials go on at me. I stick it for a year an' a half, not knowin' whether I'm comin' or goin'. Then—no more. I've had it. The wife had been tellin' me I wasn't fit to live with. 'For God's sake, turn it up, Joe,' she says. So I turn it up. First, I go in with her old man—novelties—'cos he needs somebody he can trust, bein' old an' with a bad heart. He Passes Over—then I really get goin'. I couldn't do this, I couldn't do that, couldn't I? I'd show 'em. I couldn't have this, I couldn't have that, eh? Don't make me laugh. I touched nothing I knew was pinched, but apart from that, I did what the hell I liked, had everything I wanted to have—short supply my foot! Pass the word to Joe Fettle an' he'd get it for you, at the right price. Of course the game's on its last legs, things easin' up like they are, but it'll last a bit longer yet. An' it isn't just the money, Mr. Applerose, I'll give you my word, though I can do with plenty of that; you need it runnin' this sort of business, well under the counter. But what I enjoyed was getting my own back on the blokes that told me I couldn't have this, couldn't do that."

"But aren't you running a serious risk," said Alan, "if you begin attracting attention to yourself and this place by putting out a radio programme? There'll be a hell of a row about it, you know. I'm all for it, but I warn you it can't last long. Have you thought about that?"

"Yes, but I'll take a chance. It's down my street, isn't it? Every time. An' if you an' Mr. Dobb can take chances, so can Joe Fettle. An' it's the same old carry-on, isn't it? Black coat blokes tellin' you you can't do this, can't do that. Mr. Dobb won't have it. You won't have it. An' I wouldn't have it, so I'm with you. Here, what about Miss Inga? Why isn't she on the job with us? Nice voice for the mike, I'll bet."

"I think she would have—yes. But she's quarrelled with her uncle, quarrelled with me—though I don't say I didn't ask for it."

"Don't tell me, Mr. Applerose, you're not dreamin' of her night an' day," said Fettle, with a treacly unction, as if he were about to turn himself into a crooner.

"Well, I'm not. Very attractive girl in her way, but it would never occur to me to dream of her night and day. Can't remember ever dreaming of anybody night and day."

"Don't tell the wife that, Mr. Applerose. She says it's a Romance. If she says anything, pile it on just to please her. We're goin' round for a cuppa in a minute. Hey, Mr. Dobb—want us to leave you here or are you ready for a cuppa?"

Dobb shook his head. "We've run into something here. Be round as soon as I can, Joe. You two go."

After leaving some instructions with Bert down below, Fettle drove Alan through several side-streets before stopping outside his own house. "Doesn't seem possible you're close to that transmitter here," said Alan, when they stopped. "Didn't you say you could go directly from there to here?"

"That's right. Secret way." Fettle sounded very proud of it. "Point is, Mr. Applerose, my warehouse is just at the back, only you'd never think so from outside. Proper puzzle corner it is, round here. Now come an' meet the wife."

There had been a shop on the ground level, and now it was empty and neglected. The Fettles had returned to the ancient tradition of Eastern merchants who hide their wealth behind a façade of poverty. Beyond the door at the top of the stairs was opulence, all new, polished, shining. There was too much of everything; and it seemed to have just been unpacked, the last few shavings just removed from the highly polished woodwork. The living-room was large, but even so it was not easy to move around in it, there were so many over-stuffed chairs, crowded tables, bronze elephants, giant vases, cushions, dolls, knick-knacks. There was also an ebony grand piano, like a black marble sarcophagus, bristling with silver-framed photographs and potted plants. Mrs. Fettle also seemed to have just been unpacked; she was not young, somewhere in her forties, but seemed to be newly painted and gold-plated, with everything about her hard and glittering except her eyes, which were a soft brown, melancholy, and might have belonged to a lost calf.

"Ever so pleased, Mr. Applerose," she cried; and clearly was, though her voice was as wistful and mournful as her eyes. Expecting something raucous from that dazzling and metallic appearance, he was as surprised as he would have been if he had heard the sound of a muted string quartet coming from a tank. "Now do sit up by the fire while Joe helps me with the tea. He won't let me keep a maid, and the woman's gone for the day. Sit in this chair, Mr. Applerose."

Alan did, though he would rather have sat further away from the fire, easily the largest he had seen for years; the whole room was stiflingly hot. As he sank into the deep, fat chair, he felt he would never have the energy to get out of it.

"Didn't I tell you we'd a lovely home, Mr. Applerose?" cried Fettle.

"Now, Joe, you can't talk like that." But she looked wistfully at Alan, who said it was indeed a lovely home.

"Well, you think sweet thoughts about your beautiful Young Lady," said Mrs. Fettle. Obviously as an arch sentimentalist she left her husband far behind. "Look in the fire and see if you can see your little home with Her. You like to do that, don't you?"

"No, I don't," said Alan, who was ready to oblige Fettle but felt that this was going too far.

"Go on, I'll bet you do. But perhaps you'd rather think about your music. You see, Mr. Applerose," she continued, "I know all about you. And I hope after tea you'll play us a Tune."

They brought in an enormous tea, scones dripping with butter and cream buns and chocolate cakes; Alan could not imagine where it all came from. The tea was very strong and very sweet, and he drank it with some difficulty. By the time he had drunk one cup of it, he felt so hot and sticky himself that he might have been a chocolate cake just out of the oven.

"Wouldn't it have been nice if your Young Lady could have been here?" Mrs. Fettle was almost crying with wistfulness. "Then after you could have played your Tune to Her. What does she say when you do that, Mr. Applerose?"

Feeling a fraud, Alan told her that he had never had the pleasure of playing to Miss Dobb, and that as a matter of fact he never played to anybody, not considering himself a pianist, but that if Mrs. Fettle really wanted him to try her piano he would not have the heart to refuse. To change this awkward subject, he asked Fettle about the proposed radio programme. "Dobb said you had a scheme, when I pointed out to him that I'd have to pay the musicians something."

"Do musicians bother about *money*?" cried Mrs. Fettle in horror.

"I won't deceive you, Mrs. Fettle," said Alan. "Some of 'em think about nothing else. And even the others have to live. Well, what's the scheme, Mr. Fettle?"

"Advertising," said Fettle, with a wink. "There's goin' to be a lot of fuss about Dobb's Freedom Radio, don't make no mistake about that. An' if it *does* go over big, which it can't fail, in my opinion, then some good blokes I do business with are ready to pay nice money to be mentioned."

"But they'll run into trouble. The whole thing's illegal."

"Our part is, Mr. Applerose, I grant you. But if somebody says something very nice about Smith's fish shops on the Freedom Radio, you can't blame Smith, can you? No case against him. What's he got to do with it? Let 'em try an' prove he has. No money'll change hands, mark you, Mr. Applerose. But if I get a lot of so-called damaged goods at a very cheap rate an' I know I can sell 'em at a nice price right off, then it's as good as money, isn't it?"

"I don't see it, Joe," said Mrs. Fettle. "What's the use of a lot of damaged fish?"

"Who's talkin' about fish?"

"You were. Smith's fish shops—"

"Turn it up, Beryl ducks, you're out of your depth. There aren't goin' to be fish shops. That was just a ninstance."

"I still don't follow. Do you, Mr. Applerose?"

"Yes, I see the idea. But you'll have to find somebody to put across the advertising, Mr. Fettle. I'd be no good at it—or Dobb—"

"Wouldn't dream of askin', Mr. Applerose. I've lined up a young fella—cousin of Bert's, matter of fact—an' him an' his wife's goin' to have a try. Just you do the music, Mr. Applerose."

"Well, you'll have to let me know quite soon what you're prepared to spend on the recordings. The sooner the better. I ought to get busy."

"But you *will* play me a Tune, Mr. Applerose," pleaded Mrs. Fettle. "Something nice and soft that reminds you of Her—and like those twilight melodies you do on the E.B.C.—ever so lovely, they are. Will you be able to give us anything as nice on Mr. Dobb's programme?"

"I doubt it," said Alan grimly. A few minutes later, he found himself tinkling away on the funereal grand, which was shockingly in need of tuning and had a most sluggish and sullen bass. It was easy enough, however, to improvise something that would keep Mrs. Fettle amused;

he had time and opportunity to wonder what on earth he was doing there, spinning out sugary trifles in a hellishly hot room somewhere in the dusk near Islington; and he began to go back along the chain of events that had brought him there—Stannsen's Tenth Symphony—Sir Lancelot and the E.B.C.—Dobb and his Dobbophone—

"By the way, *is* the Dobbophone here?" he asked the Fettles. "Yes, that huge thing. In his room here? Good!" He tinkled away, wondering what Inga Dobb was doing at the Hafstalmans'. Probably working it to get herself taken out for the evening by one of the Vikings. He ought to have given her a harder slap.

"You *are* thinking about your Young Lady, aren't you, Mr. Applerose?" Mrs. Fettle called out.

"I am. Or I was."

"I knew it. You had that look in your eyes. I just caught it. You see, Joe. I knew it."

Dobb came in, and Alan stopped playing at once, pleading urgent business as Mrs. Fettle protested. She disappeared with the tea things. Fettle produced whisky and soda and some superb cigars. Alan sat well back from the fire, and felt better than he had done all day.

"I admit I'm guessing," said Dobb, who looked pleased with himself. "But I'm pretty certain now I can cut in effectively, over a twenty to thirty mile radius, on any wave-length. Anyhow, I propose to try to-morrow night. Now I want you two—and your wife, Joe; and if she does it here, you must go somewhere else—to check up for me. Know anybody with a TV set in one of the suburbs, Applerose? You do? Then visit 'em to-morrow night and see what happens. I'm having a TV set up with my transmitter, so I can time my cutting in nicely. If you know somebody in a South-Western suburb, Applerose, so much the better."

Which explains why, a little later, Alan put through a call to his cousin, Enid Shutmill, who lived in Wimbledon, asking her if she would be at home the following evening, if the TV set was still working, and if he might pay his long-promised call on her and Bernard.

# CHAPTER VI

# DOBB IS HEARD

ALAN ate what he could of the blancmange and then pushed the rest of it round the glass saucer, all in a busy and happy fashion, until he saw that Enid and Bernard had finished. Then he sat back, abandoned his fork, and smiled at them. It had been one of the dreariest dinners he ever remembered, and, as he had told Inga, he preferred a couple of sandwiches in a pub to this kind of meal. Nevertheless, his smile was not altogether false. He was indeed grateful to his cousin Enid and her husband, Bernard Shutmill, who was some sort of cashier in the City, for inviting him out to Wimbledon. He knew—for they had told him—that shortly they would be joined by the Farrows from next door, and that then the five of them would sit in front of the TV set in the drawing-room. Accepting a cup of watery coffee from Enid, refusing one of Bernard's well-advertised Virginian cigarettes, lighting an Havana *bouquet finos* that Joe Fettle had given him, he regarded his host and hostess with smiling satisfaction.

These two, he reflected, were the perfect specimens of this age of mass communication and advertising. They were the copy-writer's dream. They were the circulation manager's idea of a middle-class couple. When Porton and Westfort and Mamber argued at E.B.C. Policy Meetings, they were arguing about the Shutmills. Films, newspaper headlines and feature stories, radio and TV programmes, advertising campaigns, were all aimed at Enid and Bernard, who were profoundly grateful for this attention and never failed to react properly. If an advertiser said, "Watch This Space!", they watched it. If a newspaper felt gravely concerned, then they felt gravely concerned too. The topic of the day was always their topic. If one of the E.B.C.'s parlour games was a success, then it had undoubtedly been a success with Enid and Bernard. If the Coronation had lasted for twenty-two hours on TV, they would never have taken their eyes off the screen, even at the risk of going blind and dotty. Always they did what they were told, Enid asking for *Shifto* the magic washing powder, Bernard demanding *Filter-Dung* the new cigarette. There might of course be some difference of opinion at times, when they had not been told exactly what they ought to think and feel. Thus, as Alan had learnt at dinner, Enid thought Albert Girding, the E.B.C.'s professional insulter, rather too rough and rude, whereas Bernard held that he didn't really mean it. But this gave variety and spice to life, inspiring many jolly arguments as they sat in their *All-cozee* chairs in front of the *Cheerie-Flame* gas-fire, before it was time for a cup of *Sleepo,* to guard against night famine, and then beddiebyes.

The Farrows arrived, and Raymond Farrow was balder than Bernard, and Phyllis was a trifle shorter than Enid, but otherwise there was little difference. The Farrows had a TV set too, but it was temporarily out of order, so they had ventured so far away from their own cosy fireside—not a *Cheerie-Flame* but an *Electri-Log*—so they would not miss anything and feel out of things. Alan had not had the courage to tell Enid and Bernard that he was no longer with the E.B.C., for it was this connection and not his music that brought him their interest and respect; he was proudly introduced to the Farrows as the cousin in the E.B.C. they had so often heard about. This proved to be rather awkward.

"What's happening now about this chap Dobb," said Farrow, "the chap who wouldn't play the queer instrument? Has it all been settled? Haven't heard anything about him lately."

"One of these publicity stunts," said that arch-victim of them all, Bernard, looking very shrewd and knowing. "To boost the concert you're giving—eh, Alan?"

They all looked at him, all bright and expectant. "No, it wasn't a stunt, you know," he told them. "Dobb really did refuse to play—because he'd had a quarrel with the composer, Stannsen, and they hadn't made it up. It's all quite genuine. What'll happen, I don't know."

"But, Alan, this man can't refuse to play," cried Enid, almost distressed, "when he knows very well so many important people, perhaps even royalty, are going to the concert."

"Well, he is doing," said Alan, not without satisfaction. "I don't think he cares about important people."

Bernard looked dubious. "One of the papers said he was just trying to attract attention to himself. Thinks he's an inventor, doesn't he? And I must say—that's how it looked to me." And the other three appeared to agree with him.

"It didn't to me," said Alan. "And it's damned impudence of a paper that gave him all that publicity, which he never asked for, to blame him for asking for it. However, we must wait and see what happens."

Farrow wagged a cunning finger. "I think you know more than you're telling us, old man." The ladies, feeling deliciously behind the scenes, cried their agreement. "But there are some things we all have to keep quiet about. I could tell you some pretty startling things about our business—Wholesale Drapery—but I have to keep quiet too. Safety first, eh? Quite right."

There was now some bookish talk. The Shutmills had just read the wonderful book by the young man who crossed from Where-is-it to What's-its-name in a thingummybob, and promised to lend it to the Farrows, who were just finishing the equally wonderful book by the three young men who had walked right through that terrible What-d'you-call-it jungle just to prove it was all quite safe. As Alan had to confess he had read neither of these books, was really out of touch with current literature, he suffered some loss of prestige. But his cigar was drawing well.

They settled in front of the TV set just in time to catch the last moments of an illustrated talk about fish, given by a man who looked suspiciously like an elderly carp. Nobody cared about this. Bernard kept fiddling with the set, turning the fish man into jigging lines and explosive flashes. It was the next two items that were important. The first, a notable success, one of the triumphs of the British way of life, was a kind of guessing game called "Who's Your Uncle?". It was being played, for good money and immense kudos, by a team consisting of a Fellow of Balliol, a cabaret artiste who tried to look like Little Miss Muffet, the ex-Under-Secretary to the Ministry of Social Planning, a woman novelist with a good profile and a deep voice, the head of the Brass Boiler Menders' Union, and an artful woman who was making at least five thousand a year out of being Just An Ordinary Housewife. Alan had no hope of this programme, because it was so noisy with masculine good-fellowship and winsome feminine laughter that he felt sure Dobb would not try to interrupt it. So he merely sank lower into his chair and blew smoke rings towards the screen.

There was a short interval before the next item, of which Alan had great hopes. It was a special talk by the Right Honourable Arnold Ossian-Scot, Minister of Economic Adjustment, who would explain the purpose of the new Economic Adjustment card, which would shortly be sent out to all taxpayers. He would then demonstrate how the card should be filled in by the taxpayer, before being returned to the Ministry.

"I don't think I know him," said Mrs. Farrow, passing the box of *Crunchie-Wunchies*. "Do you, Enid?"

"Isn't he the one with the long nose who was on the week before last?" said Enid. "You remember, Bernard. Have a Wunchie, Raymond?"

"Yes, that was Ossian-Scot," said Bernard. "A sound man. Very sound."

"Chap at the office, keen political type, says he's the Coming Man," said Raymond Farrow. "You run across him at all, Applerose?"

Alan said he hadn't, and, after declining a *Crunchie-Wunchie* (in spite of the fact that it was all real goodness and lovely flavour), added that he was glad of the opportunity to listen to a man of such distinction. "I'm sure I'll enjoy this," he continued hopefully.

The Rt. Hon. gent. was given quite a build-up. After an impressive announcement, by a handsome young man who looked straight into the eyes of Enid and Phyllis and smiled at them, they were shown photographs of Whitehall, Downing Street, the House of Commons, the entrance to the Ministry of Economic Adjustment, the Minister's room, while one of those urgent News Reel voices told them how important Economic Adjustment was and how busy and clever Arnold Ossian-Scot was and how we should all be talking soon about the M.E.A. cards we should have to fill up and then return to the Ministry. Then the Minister was seen at his desk, frowning at State Papers but nicely made-up for TV too. He was seen closer, but still weighed down by the cares of government. Then he suddenly looked up, caught sight of Enid and Bernard Shutmill, Phyllis and Raymond Farrow, and possibly Alan Applerose, looked for a second as if he might be sick, pulled out carefully a large false smile, then rather shakily held up the new Economic Adjustment card.

"No, it's not the one with the long nose," Enid whispered hurriedly.

Mr. Ossian-Scot pulled in the smile, cleared his throat anxiously, then said in his deepest tones, "No doubt you are all wondering what it is I am showing you. This card is something already very familiar to us in the Ministry of Economic Adjustment. Very soon it will be equally familiar to all of you who are taxpayers. You will probably follow our example and call it your *Mea Card*—M.E.A.—the initials of our ministry. Now I want you to take a closer look at this card." And immediately Ossian-Scot disappeared, and there, close up, was the card. "During the next few days," the invisible Ossian-Scot told them, sounding more confident now, "we shall be sending out many millions of these cards. They will arrive at your houses through the post. Perhaps you will find one on your breakfast table—if you take breakfast—as—er—some of us still like to do—"

Alan stirred uneasily. What was Dobb doing? Couldn't he work it after all? Was this to be a wasted evening?

They were now looking at Ossian-Scot again, rather nearer than he was before, and much more at ease, already seeing himself as one of the TV hits of the Party, with all the viewers solidly behind him.

"What do I want you to do with this card?" He paused; and then it happened.

"Tear it up," said a voice. And the voice was unquestionably the voice of Roland Dobb. Alan could have cheered. He gave a quick glance at the others, and saw that they were looking puzzled.

"First, I want you to write your full name—"

"Tear it up," Dobb commanded, his voice easily cutting through the other's quieter and less urgent tone. "Then ask these fellows why they waste your time and money on such nonsense."

"Somebody else is talking," cried Enid.

"Then your occupation," said Ossian-Scot.

"Ministries and their officials exist for our convenience," cried Dobb's voice, drowning whatever the face on the screen was mouthing. "We don't exist for their convenience."

Ossian-Scot vanished from the screen, which was occupied for a confused moment by a lot of men's shoes. Then the close-up of the card was shown again, and from somewhere behind it the Minister in an agitated tone appeared to be crying, "What? What d'you say? What is it?"

"Have we asked this fellow to send out millions of his cards?" Dobb's voice demanded. "Certainly not. Then let's teach him a lesson. Tear 'em up. Don't tell them a thing. They've all more information now than they know what to do with. We're being governed and badgered out of our minds. Stand up to these fellows."

The handsome young announcer was now back on the screen, smiling harder than ever at Enid and Phyllis. "We hope to be able to continue the talk in a few moments. There has been a technical hitch—"

"Nonsense," said Dobb. "I'm merely cutting in to give you a foretaste of Dobb's Freedom Radio, on the air with a programme next week. Don't forget—Dobb's Freedom Radio. Yes, Dobb is the name. Good-night."

Breathing hard with excitement, Bernard rushed forward and switched off the set. "You all heard it, didn't you? I think I ought to ring up and tell them. What do you say, Alan?"

"I think it's your duty, Bernard," said Alan. "Hurry up. Enid, this is important. I must get back at once. You do understand, don't you?"

"Of course, Alan. And didn't the man who interrupted call himself Dobb?"

"I thought so. Probably the same Dobb."

"Know how you feel, old man," said Farrow, who certainly didn't. "Anything I can do? Run you part of the way? Save time, y'know."

"Good of you, old man," said Alan hastily. "Just as far as the nearest Tube station, thanks very much."

"I'll get the car out." And Farrow rushed off, suddenly full of life and energy. As he said good-bye to the ladies, pink and sparkling with excitement, it occurred to Alan that Dobb was already livening them all up. Bernard was out in the hall, clinging to the telephone, still out of breath. "Number engaged all the time. Think I ought to keep trying, Alan?"

"I do, Bernard. Most important. I must run. Thanks for dinner and everything."

The night was fine but very dark when Alan came out of the Underground at the Angel. He had made a note of Joe Fettle's address, but would he ever be able to find the place? There were no taxis about; and anyhow, he felt it was time he began economizing. It took him about half an hour—after many enquiries, most of them addressed to people who hardly seemed to know they were even in London, as if they had just been dropped out of flying saucers—and it was getting on for eleven when he rang the bell outside the empty shop. However, he felt certain that Dobb and the Fettles were not the types for an early bed. He rang again, and now a light came on and he saw Joe approaching the door. For a moment they looked at each other through the grimy panel of glass.

Fettle unlocked the door and opened it about a couple of inches. "Wanting what?" he enquired cautiously. "Oh—it's you, Mr. Applerose. Come in, come in. Just wonderin' how you'd got on amongst it all. It's Mr. Applerose," he shouted from the bottom of the stairs. And as they went up, he added, still in a shout, "Now, don't give it away, don't give it away."

"Give what away?" asked Alan. They were now near the open door at the head of the stairs.

"You'll see, unless they've made a muck of it."

The sitting-room was hotter than ever. Four people were there: Mrs. Fettle, more dazzling and metallic than before in an emerald-green gown; a young man and a young woman; and a very strange figure indeed, who was sitting down and, in spite of the heat, was still wearing a hat and an overcoat. This was a most sinister-looking fellow, squinting through thick-rimmed spectacles, and with yellow wide-gapped teeth so enormous that he could not close his mouth properly; he might have been an oversize Japanese business man with a dangerously high blood pressure. As Alan gaped at this monster, Mrs. Fettle and the young woman began screaming with laughter.

"What did I tell you?" cried Fettle. "See? Works every time."

The monster nodded. All of them were laughing now. Alan wondered if he were going out of his mind. After the bright insanity of the Underground, then the gloom and confusion of the dark side-streets, a man might easily ring a bell and then find himself going through a doorway out of reality altogether.

"Good evening, Applerose," said Dobb, removing the hat and the spectacles, then whipping out the monstrous teeth.

"It's a disguise," screamed Mrs. Fettle. "Joe's idea."

Dobb was now taking off his overcoat. The young man and the young woman were introduced as Kenneth and Daphne Perman, the couple who had volunteered to do 'the commercials' on Dobb's radio programme. Fettle, as he offered drinks to the company, explained about the disguise.

"I was telling 'em," he said to Alan. "It's a nart, disguising is. Now Mr. Dobb'll have to disguise himself, straight off. So will you, I expect, Mr. Applerose, in a day or two. Now what do you do? Put on beards? That's what everybody thinks. No good, I give you my word. Spotted in a minute. Most of the blokes who have real beards look like they're disguised, don't they? I've been into all this—had to. What you want is specs, if you don't usually wear specs—an' diff'rent teeth. The teeth do it. Alters whole shape of your face—see? They wouldn't believe me—'cos they saw Mr. Dobb put 'em on. But what happened when you come in? Did you know it was Mr. Dobb? His own mother wouldn't have known him."

"She wouldn't have wanted to know him, looking like that," said Alan. "And do you mean to say that I'll have to go round soon wearing those things?"

"That's the idea," said Fettle cheerfully. "Mark you, you'll look diff'rent to Mr. Dobb. More Chineesy, I'd say. I think I've another lot somewhere. We'll try 'em on you in a minute."

"I'm not sold on this," said Alan. "If Dobb and I go out together, flashing those horrible teeth, we'll be arrested on sight." He turned on Dobb. "I came to tell you what happened to-night." And he described in detail what happened at Wimbledon. Apparently this confirmed what the others had already told him, for they had all scattered themselves to report on the effect of Dobb's cutting in. Everywhere, it seemed, the result had been equally devastating. The atmosphere was now triumphant as well as tropical. Fettle and Dobb and Alan lit cigars and drank some excellent whisky. Mrs. Fettle and the Permans preferred gin. Mrs. Fettle was for a nice Tune from Alan, but he contrived to avoid obliging her. Moving as far as he could away from the fire, he soon found himself sharing a crowded but cooler corner with the Permans, who wanted to know about the E.B.C.

Just as Enid and Bernard Shutmill were types of this Mass age, so too, Alan soon concluded, were Kenneth and Daphne Perman. They were lower-middle-class Londoners, he guessed, who by unwearying care, with a devotion worthy of a nobler cause, had transformed themselves into glamour robots. They had not yet arrived but they were most determinedly on their way up to something high above offices and shops, where they would eventually have an agent and press photographs and invitations to special nights at the Palais de Danse and the film shows, and perhaps in the end be accepted and discussed by the Shutmills and the Farrows. Everything about Kenneth and Daphne (probably including these very names) was highly artificial, studied, modelled, built up with care: their accents, manners, clothes, hair, even their style of smoking and drinking, were all part of the act. Kenneth was tall, apparently broad-shouldered and narrow-waisted, had carefully waved hair, and was vaguely good-looking, like a handsome film star seen through a wet window. Daphne was slender, dark, rather haggard in a not unpleasing fashion, and looked as if she might be photographed any minute wearing the season's new-style coat. Between them they had tried nearly everything, always just on the edge of professionalism: modelling for advertisements, ballroom dancing, crowd work in films, holiday camp entertaining, amateur hours in variety and radio, host and hostess at seaside dance hall. An odd feature of this pair was that although they were obviously devoted to each other as partners in ambition (it was easy to imagine them doing one another's hair and sponging and pressing one another's clothes), and although they existed in a world where sex was fully exploited, they somehow gave the impression of not enjoying any real sexual relationship in their marriage. Indeed, Alan, who was not given to vain fancies of this sort, soon began to feel that Daphne, flashing her smiles and for ever patting his arm, had a certain hungry look that rather alarmed him. This suspicion was confirmed by Mrs. Fettle as soon as they had gone.

"Mr. Applerose, you'll have to watch that Daphne," she cried. "Or I'll be telling your Young Lady when I meet her. Bit of a man hunter, she is, if you ask me. I was watching her. Were you Attracted?"

"No, I wasn't, Mrs. Fettle."

"I'm glad to hear it. Not in the same class as your Young Lady—"

"Now, look, we'll have to settle this. I'm sorry to disappoint you, Mrs. Fettle, but the truth is, Miss Dobb isn't my young lady. We got engaged when I was tight on Norroland schnapps—"

"I know all about that. Joe told me. But for all that, she's the One for you. Have another drink, won't you, Mr. Applerose?"

"No, thanks. If you don't mind, I'll use your telephone." He looked at Dobb and Fettle. "I'm going to ring Radio Centre, to see if Mamber's there. He's their chief publicity man. Unless I'm badly mistaken, they'll have got him on the job to-night, to answer press enquiries. Is there a phone here? Oh—under that doll, is it?" He would not have got through to Mamber's extension if the girl on PBX had not known his name. A very weary young woman answered him from Mamber's office. "Yes, you needn't tell us. We know all about it. Oh—it's you, Mr. Applerose. Yes, I'm sure Mr. Mamber would like to speak to you. Hold on."

Mamber sounded equally weary and rather hoarse. "Don't tell me you heard it, Alan. I didn't. I was dining at the Savoy, but of course they soon got hold of me. And of course all the boys have been on to us. But it won't be front page stuff unless it happens again. We're asking 'em to play it down. You heard him, did you? Then you're the very chap I want, Alan. Was it your Dobb or some other Dobb? God!—these Dobbs! Well, was it? Yes—I'll hang on, though I can't think why."

Covering the mouthpiece, Alan turned to Dobb. "He's asking if it was you—or some other Dobb," he whispered. "What do I say?"

"Tell him the same Dobb."

Alan told him. "I recognized the voice at once," he continued. "Came through very clearly."

"They'll hit the roof in the morning," said Mamber, not without a certain weary satisfaction. "Special high-level meeting at ten-thirty. *And* no bass instruments, you blighter. Boy—you wrecked that Policy Meeting all right, all right. All the papers were blown off the table, and one window went. The Air Marshal crashed in flames. Lancelot was screaming with fury—never knew he could get so high. Here—Alan—you're not in this cutting-in stunt, are you?" His voice was heavy with suspicion.

"Me, Mamber? How could I be?"

"I don't know, but I wouldn't be surprised, the games you're getting up to, these days. But if you are, take it from me, old boy, you'll be on the run shortly. They're all hopping mad here—I'm told there's even been a message from the P.M.—so watch it. 'Bye."

Mrs. Fettle, after Alan had told them what Mamber had said, announced that she was leaving them to it. While Alan and Dobb discussed the music to be recorded, Fettle disappeared for some time, and when he returned, grinning, he handed Alan a pair of thick-rimmed spectacles, with plain glass instead of lenses, and an arrangement of pink gums and large protruding teeth that looked even more horrible than those Dobb had worn. "Now try this lot for size, Mr. Applerose. I've an idea you're goin' to look very tasty."

Alan stared at himself, in the glass above the fireplace, with rising horror. "My hat! I look like a Malayan murderer. Any conscientious bobby would follow me for miles, unless he ran me in at once. I can't possibly go round looking like this. Let me try a beard. I had one once, then I got egg on it and decided it had better go."

"Why not alternate?" said Dobb, with a twinkling solemnity. "The teeth and spectacles one day, a beard the next."

Fettle wriggled appreciatively. "Well, Mr. Dobb, Mr. Applerose, we've made a nice start. I'll be talking to some of my business pals— sponsors, eh?—in the morning, after they've read the papers. An' if you want my opinion, gen'l'men, I think things'll hot up nicely very soon. Just one for the road, Mr. Applerose?"

Alan drank to their success, pocketed the horrible teeth and spectacles, and walked home, wondering when and how he would finish his *Suite for Strings*. The present atmosphere, immediate conditions, the circumstances of the moment, he concluded, were not favourable for the composition of a quiet and rather formal work.

# CHAPTER VII

# THE BEARDED LIFE

"I'M DOING it for a bet," said Alan. He was sitting in a lighted cubicle at Matelli's, the wig-maker's. Eleven o'clock on a sodden grey morning.

"In that case, sir," said the assistant, who was an Old Retainer type of man, dead right for those snobbish advertisements of soft drinks, "no doubt you'll want to wear it several days."

"Certainly," said Alan. "So please make a good job of it." Otherwise he would have to try the teeth and the spectacles. Now that Dobb's Freedom Radio was on the air and he had taken part in it, even though his name had not yet been mentioned, except as a composer, he felt himself to be almost a man on the run.

"I'll endeavour to do my best, sir. It'll take some time to fix the hair properly. I can trim the beard to your liking once the hair is in place. Now then, sir, I think we agreed that Number Nine would be the best shade. I could introduce a touch of grey, sir, if you desire it, but I wouldn't advise it, sir, unless you're thinking of greying your hair. You're not, sir? Then just lean back, sir, and raise the chin a little. Thank you, sir."

As the man began to gum on the strands of dark crepe hair, Alan had plenty of time for thought. He had plenty to think about, too. After cutting in to various E.B.C. programmes for several nights, Dobb had now launched his own programme, for which Alan had recorded some excellent chamber music, including a couple of things of his own. There had only been two nights of it so far; Alan found himself wondering if they could possibly last out the week. He and Joe Fettle doubted if they could; Dobb was more optimistic. Dobb, in fact, was altogether too optimistic, Alan thought. Dobb was enjoying himself a bit too much. The inventor in him was triumphant at the success so far of all his technical devices; the cheerful anarchist and the sardonic rebel in him rejoiced over these opportunities for speaking their minds. Only the listeners in the London area could hear him properly; but people elsewhere, as far as the ends of the earth, were being told by a large section of the press what Dobb was saying. And nobody in authority could pretend to be pleased by what Dobb said. Even the newspapers that supported authority against Dobb and took care not to report his words were at least compelled to demand that he should be silenced, pointing out that it was disgraceful that a private citizen, and such an irresponsible private citizen too, should assume the privileges of elected persons, government officials, and members of the English Broadcasting Company's staff. Where, their leader writers asked, might this end; what might be the aftermath; a grave situation, they argued, might easily develop; and they referred their readers to those famous figures of our age, the 'official spokesmen', for confirmation of these well-considered views. Meanwhile, the less responsible and more sensational papers gleefully quoted Dobb's more outrageous remarks, and described in some detail, often quite imaginary, the desperate search being made by E.B.C. engineers and the police for Dobb and his transmitter, which, they admitted, had 'certain new features' that made it surprisingly difficult to detect and locate. But the hunt was up. Dobb could not possibly get away with it much longer.

Against his own wishes, Alan found himself sharing this view. His own position was precarious. The E.B.C. associated him with Dobb; though as yet the press had said nothing about him. He had left his flat and had accepted Fettle's invitation to stay at his place, where he had a small bedroom next to Dobb's and was handy for the transmission. He had managed a couple of days of music-recording without disaster, not telling the musicians the whole story but allowing them to guess he was up to something fishy (they were all rebellious types, good Dobb men, anyhow); but after that he had had to keep under cover, and had soon had more than enough of it, if only because Mrs. Fettle's cuisine had its limitations: hence this dash down to Matelli's. For the nightmare teeth-and-spectacle disguise just would not do, whatever Joe Fettle might say. A beard was the thing; and now, as he kept glancing at himself in the well-lighted mirror, he saw it taking shape, strand by strand, and his own familiar looks vanishing behind it.

"There you are, sir," said the Old Retainer, regarding his creation with approval. "Looks as if it had grown on you. Undetectable in any ordinary circumstances, sir. Pass anywhere."

"Except that I look like a young Druid—or a minor Dostoevsky character," said Alan, scowling at the hirsute image, which scowled back at him in the most alarming manner.

"Ah—but now for the trim, sir. We oughtn't to rush this, sir, if you'll allow me to say so. What had you in mind, sir? Not too full, I'd say. Attracts more attention—of the wrong kind, sir—and, in my opinion, wouldn't suit you as well as something a bit finer. I'd suggest something between the Sea Captain and the fairly full Vandyke—something artistic about 1900, I'd say—"

"With just a hint of the Mephistophelean, perhaps," said Alan, now entering into the spirit of the enterprise. "Start trimming, then. I'll tell you when to stop. Take it easy, though."

The progression was fascinating. *Druid-moujik-vegetarian-religious-crackpot* gave place to *professional-man-circa* 1865, who in turn was transformed into *youngish-master-mariner*-1885, who only needed a few more snips of the scissors to become *new-Academician ("Won't Oo Kiss My Doggie?"—hung on the line)* 1898; and now every quarter of an inch of hair was important. Snip—steady now—snip! "Enough," cried Alan; and put a hand up to the sheet that covered his shoulders. The Old Retainer removed the sheet triumphantly.

Alan stared, fascinated and not without awe, at the mysterious dark devil of a fellow in the mirror. There was a man capable of anything except a decent life in Wimbledon alongside the Shutmills and the Farrows. He flashed a grin at the fellow, who replied, teeth and eyes glittering, with a diabolical smile. Here was a man known to every dive between Macao and Tangier; impossible to imagine him working for the E.B.C. or looking in at the Royal College of Music.

"What if it gets wet?" he enquired rather anxiously.

"It would be as well to take reasonable precautions," replied the old retainer magician. "Do you carry an umbrella, sir?"

"I don't. And I'm certain this chap wouldn't. Black oilskins and a swordstick, probably. I'll have to try to keep out of the rain—or tuck it in. I'll look in again if it shows signs of moulting." He paid his bill, and, feeling rather self-conscious, marched off towards Shaftesbury Avenue. After a few minutes, during which he put on a slight swagger, he began to feel aggrieved because nobody seemed to be giving him a second glance.

Nevertheless, he decided against going to his usual pub, near

Radio Centre. That was too risky. So he went the other way and finally entered a large saloon bar not far from the Coliseum. It was fairly full, with minor theatrical types most prominent, and across the curved bar he noticed two 'cellists he had conducted several times. After he had obtained a beer and a couple of sandwiches, he took courage and began boldly staring about him. Some of the girls, he fancied, returned his glances encouragingly, either widening or narrowing their eyes according to their respective techniques. A smile or two— of admiration not derision—came his way. All this was gratifying, not because he wanted to know any of these girls but because their reaction confirmed his view of this bearded disguise, undoubtedly he looked a devil of a fellow, not at all like Alan Applerose. And then, through a gap in a group, he noticed above a table against the wall a heavy Teutonic face that he had seen before. Could it be? It was. There, not four yards away, was Herr Julius Grobemeier, of Mannheim, master of the *Great-German-Double-Bombardon*.

He edged past the group, who seemed to be arguing about Dobb, until he was quite close to Herr Grobemeier's table. Yes, the other three were there—Signor Nicola Bertini, of Milan, and Alfred and Louis Sauvager, of Clermont-Ferrand—all four of them huddled together, looking very melancholy, rather as if they found themselves sitting at the bottom of the sea. With them, their host apparently on a very modest, almost parsimonious, scale, was a little fat man in a horrible striped suit much too small for him. And this little fat man was hot and excited, nearly out of his mind trying to make them understand, to conquer their vast apathy and melancholy. Alan edged nearer still. The little fat man was almost crying.

"Now listen—just listen, for God's sake." He was using that loud tone, suitable for a deaf idiot, that passes as a foreign language with many English. "My cousin—cousin—father's brother's son—twiggy voo?—is with the E.B.C. at Radio Centre. E.B.C.—Radio Centre— comprenny? He sees you there that afternoon. He rings me up— telephone—get me?" He did a fine little miming turn of a man telephoning. "He says to me, 'Charlie,' he says, 'there's an act there, if you built it up right. An' you could do it, Charlie, nobody better,' he says. So that's what I'm talking about, messoos. An act," he shouted in despair. "For variety. A variety act. All four of you. With them instruments of course. Get me? Act. Variety."

Herr Grobemeier and Signor Bertini stared at him sadly. The

brothers Sauvager broke out together in a passionate spate of highly idiomatic French of which Alan hardly caught a word. For the moment, however, the little man forgot his despair.

"That's just what I want. You two big blokes not saying a word, an' these two goin' at it hell for leather. You'd murder 'em, honest you would. What an act!"

"Eesa radio deesa act?" said Signor Bertini.

"There y'are—talk English good as I can," cried the little fat man triumphantly.

But now Signor Bertini looked blank again. Herr Grobemeier might have been a tub of lard. As for Alfred and Louis, their outburst seemed to have exhausted them, and now not only were they silent again and sad, but they appeared to have shrunk, to be all melancholy monkey eyes and unreal moustaches.

The little fat man looked at them, ran a finger round the inside of his damp collar, and tried once more, "Variety—comprenny? Music hall."

Herr Grobemeier nearly came to life. "Ja—ja. Museeg holl. Vaudeville."

"Now you've got it, messoo. An act. Variety act. I Could Build You Four Into A Good Act—"

It was at this point that Alan felt certain that somebody was staring hard at him. He looked around. The rather raffish-looking girl sitting two tables away had bold dark eyes, and it was these eyes that were staring very hard at him. Then he saw them light up with jubilant recognition. As he turned away hastily, he remembered where and when he had seen the girl before, and who she was. It was the woman journalist who had burst into his room at Radio Centre with the middle-aged newspaperman, the day the Dobb story broke. They were the pair who had had the nerve to borrow instrument cases. Yes, and he remembered her name now—Helen Mick, of the *Morning Star*—an impudent wench, the man had called her. As he neared the counter, to put down his glass, he risked another look round. She had risen; she was moving towards him; in another minute she would be shouting his name. He squirmed through a solid gang at the end of the bar, dashed into the street, and jumped into a taxi. That had been a close thing. Evidently the beard would not deceive everybody; though women journalists who were also impudent wenches were probably somewhere at the top, far above Scotland

Yard, when it came to penetrating disguises.

Mrs. Fettle admired the beard and said it made him look so handsome and dashing that he ought to grow a real one. But when he told her about Helen Mick, she was not surprised. "You ought to have some different clothes to go with it. Women notice clothes, remember, even men's clothes. I'll bet you were wearing just the same things when she saw you before. Why don't you slip down to a good second-hand place and buy some things that match that beard? No— listen—I'll go. What are your sizes?"

Before she returned, while he was developing an amusing little theme at the piano, Joe Fettle came in, looking worried. Joe admired the beard too, but he still looked worried. Alan asked him if anything was wrong.

"Well, for one thing," said Fettle, wriggling hard, "Kenneth Perman's off. Got 'flu or something, so he's gone back to his mother to enjoy it. Always goes back to his mother when he's off colour, Daphne says. An' that's another thing—Daphne. She's nuts on you— you know that, don't you? The wife spotted it right off, first time you met. An' that beard won't cool her off neither." He looked anxiously at Alan.

"I can't see why that should worry you, Joe."

"Play her up a bit, Alan boy," said Fettle, dropping his voice. "She could do nicely for herself if she gave us away. Get herself in the papers an' all that, an' you know what she is—on the make. So don't let her feel dissatisfied, play her up. Specially to-night."

"Why specially to-night?"

Joe looked uncomfortable. "Reasons."

"You'll have to do better than that, Joe. Come on, now. You're looking terribly shifty."

"Now look, Alan boy, I'd rather not say. 'Cos if you don't know, she can't get it out of you, can she? It's the wife's idea as well as mine. It's going to be tricky to-night after we finish, an' we're stoppin' at half-past nine sharp. Very tricky. So it's up to you to bring her back here an' keep her sweet for an hour or two. Don't let her go or she might shop us just at the wrong time—"

"What is all this?" cried Alan, irritated. "What's going to be tricky?"

"Now don't spoil it, Alan. I've got it all worked out nicely—you mightn't think it but I'm a hell of a norganizer, I am—I've had to be in my game. No, don't ask no more questions. I'll tell you this much. Mr. Dobb won't believe it—though I've made him give in at the finish—but they're closin' in on us. Don't kid yourself they're not. I've had my boys scattered round, askin' questions on the quiet, an' they all say the same thing. We haven't much time. That's why it's goin' to be tricky. An' don't worry about Mr. Dobb an' me an' the wife to-night. We'll be busy. Just you keep Daphne amused—that'll be your share. Now promise, Alan boy."

He was so much in earnest that Alan, though still bewildered, said he would do what he could to entertain Daphne after the broadcast. And before he could ask any more questions, Mrs. Fettle returned triumphantly with the clothes she had bought for him. They consisted of a pair of blue whipcord trousers, a golden-brown corduroy jacket, a dark brown woollen shirt, and an apple-green tie. She insisted on his wearing them at once. When he came down in all their glory, she screamed her admiration. "You look a one and no mistake. It's a good job Joe's here or I'd be having a go at you myself. Have you told him about that Daphne, Joe?"

"He knows, ducks. Promised to do his best."

"Ask why she isn't happy," said Mrs. Fettle. "That'll keep her going some time. It always did me. I'd be good for an hour of it even now. Well, Joe an' me's goin' to be busy, so you go up and have a nice rest, Alan. We'll have a big high tea about six and there'll be some drinks an' sandwiches for you after the broadcast. Tell Mr. Dobb to be down here at six, Joe."

At half-past seven, Dobb, Joe, Alan and Daphne (who was already holding on to Alan's arm) went upstairs to an attic, entered what appeared to be a large wardrobe—it had a false back that admitted them into the top floor of the next building, also owned by Joe—then crossed a long empty room, which had an entrance, through a cupboard, into the room where the transmitter was. All three men took a boyish delight in these secret entrances and exits; only Daphne, whose mind was fixed on other things, thought them silly. The gadgets were tested; the brief scripts looked over; and at eight o'clock they were on the air.

"This is Dobb's Freedom Radio," Dobb announced in an easy style, "with an hour and a half of comment and music. And this is Roland Dobb speaking. Some of you are wondering, I'm told, why we're doing this. Do we imagine that we're better at radio programmes than the experts of the E.B.C.? The answer is *No*. We make no claims of that sort. We're doing it chiefly to show that it can be done. We don't do anything like enough for ourselves nowadays. We depend far too much on politicians and officials, with the result that they have too much power. This is bad for them and bad for us. As you may see by taking a look at the world. Men who are always wanting power shouldn't have it. And ordinary citizens should insist upon controlling their own lives. We're not babies, though there's a danger that soon there might be very few real adults left. One newspaper, which has always been wrong about everything, suggests I do this because I like the sound of my own voice. Possibly I do, but I consider I've as much right to air my opinions as the proprietor of that newspaper has—and I do it more openly and honestly. I'm also told that the Government are very angry about this broadcasting. Well, that makes a nice change for some of us—me, for instance. I used to be angry when they were pleased with themselves. Now for once I'm pleased with myself and they're angry. I'll talk to you again, later. Meanwhile, there's a young lady here who has something to say to you. Yes, Daphne?"

"I've had rather an exciting day to-day, Mr. Dobb," cried Daphne winsomely into the mike. And then, within the framework of a shopping expedition, she introduced the names of certain products manufactured or sold by some of Joe's business pals. Kenneth should have followed her, doing the same sort of thing for male listeners, but to-night Alan had to read the script, which had been put together by Daphne and Joe and proved to be an awkward and embarrassing specimen of English prose. However, Alan, who had done a certain amount of emergency announcing at E.B.C. concerts and recitals and was not afraid of the mike, struggled through it somehow, though never achieving Kenneth's holiday camp chumminess or Palais de Danse gentility, and never succeeding in sounding as if he believed a word he said. Then he gave them some of the music he had recorded; Dobb read out some news items, with sardonic comments; Daphne did some more winsome advertising; then more music and finally there was a Good-night talk from Dobb, who on this occasion took politicians as his topic.

"The older I get," said Dobb, "the less I like 'em. They're miles out of their place now. Once they did a job and didn't pretend to be better than the rest of us—or if they did, nobody believed 'em. Now we take 'em at their own valuation. All-round wise men, who know how we ought to lead our own lives better than we do. How they learnt so much, making speeches and plotting in smoke rooms, beats me. I can't for the life of me see how a man who's spent most of his time jockeying for power is supposed to have acquired so much wisdom. Part of the trick of course is for them to make us feel helpless, then to promise to get us out of the mess that they in fact got us into. Unfortunately too many people play up to this, ask for it. They've stopped thinking for themselves, stopped taking any action for themselves. Without a murmur they allow politicians and their officials to do things to them that our grandfathers would never have tolerated for a moment. Governments have been pulled down, ministers chased out of their offices, for doing things that are accepted now without a protest. You want an example? Here's one. When I was young the only countries in Europe that had the passport system were Russia and Turkey, both considered out of date and tyrannical. Now we all have it clamped on us. Have we asked for it? No. Do we like it? No. But we still have it. Do passports trap international crooks? No—they have dozens of passports; there's a trade in 'em in places like Tangier. Governments like passports because they give them a complete stranglehold on their citizens. Take away a man's passport and, unless he's a crook and knows all the dodges, he's helpless. And politicians like to see people helpless. It increases their sense of power. And don't be taken in by the sham fights they have among themselves. They all want to behave in much the same way. They're against you, not against each other, except when they're jockeying round for places. The ones who are out say they're going to be better next time, when they're in again; but they never are, they're always worse. We live in a world where thousands of millions of pounds are being spent on destructive machinery and idiotic explosions, and yet it's harder and harder to get a mutton chop. Is this the world ordinary people want? Not on your life. It's been created by the ambition, vanity and stupidity of political leaders. What about some meetings on a high level? We've had them, and much good they've done us. What we need are plenty of meetings on a low level, between sensible people who aren't eaten up by a love of power, the very people who now can't cross a frontier, spend their own money as they please, go and do what they like where they like, the people who foot the bill but aren't even allowed to look at the menu. Good-night."

They were off the air. As a rule, feeling suddenly relaxed, they began gossiping about the night's programme; but to-night the atmosphere was quite different, as Alan noticed at once. Dobb and his silent man, Ted, began doing things to the apparatus. Joe gave Alan an impatient nudge, and, when he turned, Joe flicked a thumb in the direction of Daphne, who was examining her make-up.

"Come on, Daphne," said Alan. "We'll go down."

"Just us?"

"Yes. Drinks and sandwiches. We've earned 'em."

"Suits me, sweetie." She squeezed his arm. "What about Mrs. Fettle? She'll be there."

"I gather she won't. And don't ask me why, Daphne, because I don't know."

"I couldn't care less. She doesn't like me, and I'm not mad about her. Heavenly stuff your coat's made out of — I love the feel of it." She chattered all the way across and down to the Fettles' sitting-room. "Isn't it a scream Kenneth always running back to his mother as soon as he thinks he's ill? As if I couldn't look after him! But I must say, he's better off with his mother — she's in more than I am. Makes a nice change for me too. Kenneth's a bit much at times. Hasn't much sense of yumour, y'know, Kenneth hasn't. Not like you. I'll bet you've a lovely sense of yumour, haven't you?"

"No, I don't think so," said Alan carefully. "I wouldn't say I'd much of a sense of humour."

This confession astounded Daphne, who had probably been surrounded for years by people kept going only by their magnificent senses of humour. She decided he was teasing her; she then put in some arch rallying work, which took them into the sitting-room. "Nice and cosy in here to-night," she added appreciatively.

It seemed to Alan rather like a cluttered-up blast furnace, but, remembering what Joe had said about keeping her there for an hour or two, he did not venture to disagree. He gave her the gin-and-tonic she asked for, and passed the sandwiches. No sooner had he taken a drink himself than Mrs. Fettle looked in. "No, I'm not joining you, I'm going to be busy for some time. Enjoy yourselves. What I wanted to say was — keep this door closed, by all means, but don't shut the door that gives on to the stairs — or the one down below. Cheeri-bye!"

"All right by me so long as we haven't to keep this door open," said Daphne. "But what's she up to? No, I know, you haven't a clue — you've told me, and for once I believe you. What about turning off that middle light? Make it look cosier, wouldn't it? I must say, you ought to grow a real beard like that. You looked pretty good before but now you're absolutely smashing. How do I look? I put on this thing just for your benefit."

"You look wonderful," cried Alan. This was not true, but she certainly looked very trim and pretty.

"Well, well, well! Now we are hearing something. Do you really mean it? All right, then. Kiss me."

"I'm dying to," said Alan, remembering his instructions. It was too early, though, to start kissing. Keep the kisses, he decided, for when all else had failed. "But I want you to tell me something first. It's been worrying me, Daphne." He went a little closer and stared into her eyes. "Here you are—a ravishingly pretty girl, smart, clever, ready to make a big name for yourself—and yet I feel you're not happy. Why are you unhappy, Daphne dear?"

Mrs. Fettle had been quite right; this worked like magic. Daphne smiled a sad little smile; her eyes misted over with self-pity. "You might well ask that, Alan darling. Sit down here and make yourself comfortable. That's better. Why aren't I happy. Yes, that's the question, isn't it? That's what I ask myself. I know I've got a lot, more than most girls. Including Kenneth, who may be maddening—poor sweet—but still adores me. I ask myself what I want." She opened her eyes very wide and stared at the vanishing blue hills of felicity. "A lot of things, of course—but they're just ordinary things. Some people think I'm hard. I'm not really hard—*you* must know that, and if you knew me better, you'd know it better—but I have to act a part with people like that. To protect myself. I don't want *them* to see me as I really am. With somebody like you, it's different. *You're* different—just as I'm different." She laid a hand on his. "It just isn't true I only want to take a lot. I want to give a lot too. To be my true self with somebody who really understands. To—"

But then Helen Mick of the *Morning Star* marched in, smiling, triumphant. Alan jumped up to stare, Daphne to glare.

"Intruding, I'd say," cried Miss Mick, without any suggestion of an apology. "But I'm working, though ready to stop and play at the drop of a hat. We meet again, Mr. Applerose."

"I zeenk you mak' a beeg mistak'," said Alan, hoping against hope.

"I zeenk not—'ow you say," said Miss Mick coolly. "I recognized you in that pub this morning, and you know it. Though I must admit the get-up to-night is even more in character and more smashing. My God—you look attractive in that beard, Applerose. I suppose she's just been telling you that."

"Who is this woman?" demanded Daphne haughtily, rather like a duchess in a musical comedy, Number Two tour.

"Oh, I'm sorry. Miss Helen Mick, of the *Morning Star*—Mrs. Daphne Perman." They exchanged the smallest and coldest smiles Alan had ever seen; it was two Snow Queens meeting at the North Pole.

"And Daphne who does the corny advertising on the Dobb programme, I'd add," said Miss Mick, tossing her coat on the grand piano, where it knocked over six silver-mounted photographs. "You keep it very hot in here, don't you? And that isn't a crack, though I see how it could be. A drink, please, Applerose. Gin and ginger ale, I think."

Remembering what Joe had told him about things being very tricky for the next hour or two, Alan's reflections, as he mixed the drink, were sombre and fearful. Now he had two of them on his hands, and Helen Mick must be even more dangerous than Daphne. She had already discovered where he was. What else had she discovered?

"I'm wondering how you found out I was here." He handed her the drink. Both women were now sitting down, deep in the overstuffed chairs, like armies preparing for trench warfare. They both had cigarettes going and were contemptuously blowing smoke across at each other.

"It was a long shot," said Miss Mick. "I've been in constant touch with the Dobb girl for my paper—we're trying to get a story about her uncle out of her, but so far she won't play—and she told me about these Fettles. I've been combing this district for the last hour trying to find this place. All the doors were open below, so I walked in. *Et—voilà*—as you Frenchmen say. And I'll tell you another thing, poppet. It's not long since you finished the broadcast. Therefore, you must have your little studio not too far from here. How do you like that, my bearded sugar-plum?"

"I don't like it at all," Alan confessed. It was now clear that Helen Mick must be encouraged to stay as long as possible; she was far more dangerous than Daphne. He smiled at her.

"I must say you're madly attractive," cried Miss Mick. "Don't you think so, Mrs.—er—?"

"I haven't given it a thought," said Daphne coldly. "Mr. Applerose and I happen to have some important business to discuss."

"That's what I gathered when I burst in on you," said Miss Mick. "Well, if you want my opinion, people, I think the game's up. They're all hot on the trail. It's probably only a matter of hours now. Tewson of the *Post*, for instance, a very smart boy, told me this afternoon he'd find Dobb within twenty-four hours. And then of course there's the police, who are probably working on it like mad but won't tell us anything. No, children, you've had it. Pass me a sandwich, please, Applerose darling. I just peck at proper meals but I can never resist sandwiches. Ham, too. Divine."

There was a silence, which Miss Mick, busy with the sandwiches, seemed to enjoy. Daphne continued to glare at her. Alan tried to think of a subject that both ladies might like to discuss. Nothing suitable suggested itself. He lit one of Joe's fine cigars.

Finally, Daphne, behaving now as if Miss Mick were not there, broke the silence. "As I was saying," she began, "if it comes, as I think it will, to a choice between TV and films, I shan't know what to say. What do *you* think, Alan dear?"

"I don't know," said Alan, who certainly didn't.

"I'd just say *Yes*," said Miss Mick, not very convincing as a sweetly helpful friend. "Or do you find that too difficult?"

Like one descending from great heights to observe the insect world, Daphne now recognized Miss Mick's existence. "We're discussing something rather important, if you don't mind."

"*You* may be," said Miss Mick cheerfully, "but he isn't. I can tell by the look on his face—bless him—that he hasn't the least idea what you're talking about. Let's change the subject, if it ever was one. Where did you get that peculiar rigout, Applerose?"

"I think it's charming," said Daphne hastily.

"Not my choice, I must admit," said Alan, wondering if there was safety here. "The coat's not bad—but the shirt and the tie are a bit fierce, aren't they?"

Miss Mick looked him over with those bold dark eyes of hers. "What about a floppy big bow—early Montmartre style? Stand up. Let me see if I can tie one."

The next moment, he was standing up, she was standing up, very close to him; and the moment after that, Daphne was standing up too, equally close to him on the other side. There followed some competing business with the tie, each girl being sharply dissatisfied with the efforts of the other, and each of them leaning heavily against him while she watched and criticised the other girl. And then, with his tie hanging loose and his hair all ruffled by various bits of feminine playfulness, he seemed to have the pair of them competing to wind their arms about him. Which was all very well, not unpleasant in itself and passing the time nicely; but unfortunately it was then that Inga Dobb arrived.

"Oh—I'm sorry," she cried, seeing the two girls embracing a strange bearded man. But then, moving closer, she recognized Alan; and apologies were out. "Although I'm not really on speaking terms with either you or Uncle Roland," she told him severely. "I came to warn you. I mean, about the newspaper people and the police. But I didn't expect to find you wearing a beard and a fancy coat, with two girls round your neck—"

"They were trying to tie my tie in a different way," Alan began. He saw, rather to his surprise, that she really was a bewitching girl. The other two hadn't a chance beside her. "Miss Inga Dobb—Mrs. Daphne Perman. Miss Mick you know, I gather. Yes, they were tying my tie—"

"As soon as I saw that little wart thing on the left side of your nose, I knew it was you." She looked with marked disapproval at Daphne. "Mr. Applerose and I used to be engaged, but I broke it off."

"Is that so?" said Daphne haughtily. "I'm married to Kenneth Perman—you must have heard about him—"

"No, I haven't," said Inga.

"Very good-looking, very clever, lots of charm and personality," Daphne continued, as if recommending Kenneth for a job. "Don't you agree, Alan darling?"

"Oh—certainly—certainly." Alan did his best. "Will you have a drink, Inga?"

"No, thank you. But I'm sure these ladies would like some more."

"This lady would," cried Miss Mick, "and will now help herself. Anybody join me? You, Daphne? And for God's sake, stop looking as if you'd just been insulted—it's so boring."

"Perhaps you're more used to it than I am," said Daphne, still wounded.

"Nobody could be more used to it than I am," said Miss Mick cheerfully. "You could make nice strong luggage out of my skin. I must say, Miss Dobb, I thought your Boy Friend here very attractive the first time I met him, but now with this beard he's fiendishly devastating. If you don't want him, then I do."

"I don't think you're his type, Miss Mick," said Inga thoughtfully. She took a sandwich. "I'm half a Norrolander, as you know, and now that I'm staying with Norroland friends, I see a lot of Norroland men. They're mostly very big and fair. I think they're very attractive." She bit the sandwich and looked across at Alan with wide smiling innocence.

"No, you don't," said Alan. "Otherwise, you'd have nobbled one. The truth is, you're bored with 'em. How's Hafstalman?"

"Very well. And how's Uncle Roland? And why isn't he here?"

"He's very lively. And why should he be here?" He gave her a warning glance, and indicated Miss Mick, whose back was turned to them.

Inga nodded. "I knew he came to see Joe Fettle sometimes. And where are the Fettles? I came to see the Fettles. It never occurred to me you'd be here, smothered in girls."

"Alan, darling," cried Daphne, "I'd better do your tie for you now, hadn't I?"

"Surely you're not going to start all that again, Mrs. Perman," said Inga severely. "Not that I'm staying long, if Mr. and Mrs. Fettle aren't here."

"Well, *I'm* going in a minute or two," said Daphne.

"And so is Aunty Helen, children," said Miss Mick. "Though this devastating Applerose, with or without beard, is more than welcome to come with me."

"My uncle would be furious," said Inga, "if he knew Mr. Applerose was wandering about London with a journalist. He would think it quite treacherous. Particularly as you're not at all to be trusted, Miss Mick. You know you shouldn't be here at all. After pretending to be so sympathetic to my uncle, when you wanted me to write something about him, you're trying to track him down. I'm furious with you. I'll never tell you anything again."

Miss Mick merely grinned. "Stop it, young 'un. The heavily reproachful isn't your line. Besides, I'm working for a living. If the *Morning Star* wants Dobb, I'm after him, and I don't care whose uncle he is. You make big eyes at this young man of yours, before Daphne here gets her claws into him."

"I beg your pardon," Daphne began, loftily.

"And I beg yours," said the man who entered at that moment. He was both tall and wide; his features were huddled together in his meaty face so that it had large blank spaces all round them; he wore a dark blue raincoat and carried a bowler. Alan knew at once that he was a policeman of some sort. This looked like being game-and-set.

"I'm a police officer—Inspector Filer. Would you mind giving me your names?" He took out a note-book, sat down, and immediately began to sweat. "Keep it warm in here, don't you?" He looked at Alan. "Your name, please."

"Bernard Montgomery. No relation to the Field-Marshal," Alan added earnestly. "That's just a coincidence. A nuisance at times, too. I'm a percussion player, but not working at the moment. Actually I'm looking for a good pair of cymbals—but they're harder and harder to find—"

Inspector Filer shook his head impatiently, and Alan thought he saw drops fly off his face, which now looked like wet steak. "And your name, young lady?" said the inspector to Inga.

"Erika Greta Trockmanssen," said Inga in a peculiar accent. "I am Norrolander, you see, please."

Instead of writing down this difficult name, the inspector mopped his face. He then learnt that Daphne was a Mrs. Batchworth, staying with an aunt in Willesden, and that Miss Mick was a Miss Marjorie Pearson, who taught geography in a girls' school at Penge.

"Well, that's that," said the inspector, not sounding very happy. "Now I understand that a Mr. and Mrs. Fettle live here. Where are they, Mr. Montgomery?"

"I don't know, Inspector," said Alan truthfully. "They told me to make myself at home here for an hour or so, while they attended to some business, so I've been entertaining these ladies, all friends of mine. You wouldn't like a drink?"

"I would, but I'm not having one. I'm on duty."

"May I ask—what duty? We're delighted to see you, of course—"

The ladies murmured their agreement, gave him soft looks, smiled at him.

"We have reason to believe," said Inspector Filer, who was now nearly steaming, "that illegal radio transmission is taking place in or close to these premises. A very serious offence indeed. And I'd strongly advise you, Mr. Montgomery, and these ladies too, not to withhold any information in your possession concerning this matter, because the authorities are taking a grave view of it — a very grave view. I think I'd better have half a glass of soda water, if it's all the same to you, Mr. Montgomery. Oppressive in here. Thank *you*, Mr. Montgomery." He drank the soda water, still keeping an eye on them. His face was rather foolish, with so much blank meat on it, but he had a sharp little eye, not unlike an elephant's. "And because the authorities take such a grave view, I've been given what you might call a general warrant. I can search any premises I think suspicious. So now I'm going to have a look round here. Anybody like to come with me? Always glad of a witness."

Inga and Miss Mick offered to accompany him. After a panic-stricken look at Alan, Daphne hastily announced that she must go home. Alan hesitated; but with the inspector's eye on him, he felt he ought to bluff it out. So Daphne hurriedly departed, and the other three fell in behind the inspector. When they went up to the top floor, Inga dug her nails into Alan's palm to show that she understood and sympathised.

Inspector Filer soon proved that he was not as stupid as he had at first appeared to be. After one sharp look round in the attic, he walked straight across to the false wardrobe. "People ought to remember they leave marks on a floor," he said, pointing.

"This is exciting," cried Miss Mick.

"Yes, isn't it?" said Alan as cheerfully as he could. Inga nipped his arm to show that she too knew that now the situation was very dangerous indeed.

"Neat," said the inspector, indicating the false back that opened into the next attic, "but I've seen 'em before. Hello — who are you?"

Alan had a shock. Here was Joe Fettle, wearing a huge check overcoat and a green pork-pie hat at the back of his head, grinning and wriggling away. "Havin' a look round?" he enquired pleasantly. "That's right — Fettle's the name."

The inspector explained who he was and what he was up to, and then went into a cat-with-mouse act that would have been effective if Joe had been content to play the mouse. "What I'm wondering, Mr. Fettle," he said, almost making a purring sound, "is why you rigged up this contraption and why so many people seem to have been coming this way. Got any ideas for me, Mr. Fettle?"

"Certainly," said Joe promptly, to Alan's astonishment. "We go through there to the next top floor. Then we go through a cupboard to the next place. Come on, I'll show you. Take a bit of pride in it, I do. Ask the wife, who laughs at me. This way. Mind your head, Inspector."

"I adore this," Miss Mick announced, and was enthusiastically supported by Miss Dobb. The inspector breathed heavily; Alan almost stopped breathing; Joe, now leading the way, hummed one of the cockney songs of his youth.

Alan saw at once, what he ought to have guessed earlier, that Dobb's radio room had been thoroughly cleared out, though there was still something, bulky and wrapped in old cloths, where the transmitting apparatus had been. The inspector pointed at it, permitting himself now a broad grin. "You're a cool card, Mr. Fettle, and it was as nice a piece of bluffing as I've struck lately. But I fancy that's what I'm after."

"Is that so?" said Joe, with apparent anxiety. "Seemed all right to me, Inspector. I bought it cheap, I'll admit, but from a good old firm— no funny business about 'em. Had it put together up here so my mechanic could have a good go at it. However, you take a look— an' let me know if you think there's been any hanky-panky." He was now taking the cloths off the machine. "It stamps out soles an' heels— Swiss job originally, they told me. Out of my usual line, of course, but it was goin' cheap an' I thought it might be a good spec'. There you are. Wants a good clean up."

The inspector stared with disgust at the machine, which might or might not stamp out soles and heels but was obviously no part of any possible radio apparatus. "All right, cover it up. But I'd like to know why you have to do all this fancy secret-door work, Mr. Fettle. Very peculiar, to say the least of it."

"Yuman nature, that's all," said Joe cheerfully. "Look—I work in this buildin'—live in the other one. Right? Right. I buy things. I sell 'em. Try to make a profit. Well, after a time, it's dull. I'm like a kid. I want to work up a bit of excitement. So what do I do? I fool around with them cupboards an' wardrobes. I come this way to work just to give it a fancy touch—"

"I'm not surprised," said Alan. "You're a Romantic, Joe. Always knew it."

"So did I," cried Miss Dobb. "And I think you're sweet, Mr. Fettle. Don't you think so, Miss—er—?"

"Not quite my idea of a sugar-plum, dear," said Miss Mick. "But I see what you mean."

Inspector Filer looked at them all with disgust. "Well, let's go."

When they finally returned to the sitting-room the inspector picked up his bowler and looked slowly from one to the other of them. "Well, I'm off. But before you start slapping each other on the back, I'll tell you one or two things, just to show you I'm not as silly as I look. First, you, Fettle. I didn't believe a word of your yarn. That room up there had just been cleaned out. No—don't argue. We'll leave it at that." He turned to Alan. "I don't know what you're up to—and you might be looking for a good pair of cymbals. But I don't see how a false beard's going to help." He looked at the girls. "You don't teach geography anywhere," he told Miss Mick. "You're on a newspaper, though I've forgotten which. I'll give you a lift, then you can tell me. As for you, young lady—" he wagged a fat forefinger at Inga—"next time you start off with a foreign accent, remember to keep it up. You forgot it upstairs. Coming?" he said to Miss Mick, who nodded and smiled sweetly and followed him out.

"I thought he was such a stupid man," said Inga. "Big fat men always look so stupid."

"That's the idea," said Joe. "There's two or three of 'em like him. They get to the top just by lookin' soft an' silly. An' that one's rumbled us all right—only of course he's got no evidence. Well, Alan boy, I told you it'ud be tricky—but I worked it just in time. Organization did it—I'd everything worked out marvellous. Had another place all ready, you bet your life. Mr. Dobb an' the tackle's up there now. Me an' the wife's been up there an' come back. Question now is—do we move in up there or stick it here, riskin' bein' followed? Tricky either way."

Mrs. Fettle came in, carrying a tea-tray; she greeted Inga with enthusiasm; and the two of them went off into a corner to chatter over their tea-cups. Alan and Joe helped themselves to whisky and remained close to the decanter.

"Where is this place, then?" asked Alan.

"Finsbury Park way," said Joe, out of the side of his mouth. "It's called the Metropolitan Dramatic an' Music Academy. Come down in the world—if it was ever up. They've still got the bottom floor, I've taken the rest. This professor bloke who runs it doesn't know what we're doin'—I told him we're experimentin'. The poor old sausage hasn't a clue. There's a sort of flat—not much furniture but enough to eat an' sleep on. You pack a bag, Alan boy, an' I'll run you up there shortly."

"It's a risk, isn't it, Joe? Won't the police be keeping watch?"

"They are. I know it. But down here, not outside the Union Jack Novelty Company where I've left the car. An' we'll go over the top an' down through the warehouse an' out that way."

"What about Daphne?"

"She's out. Daren't risk tellin' her about this new place. I'll phone her in the mornin'. I've told the wife she can have a go doin' Daphne's stuff—"

He was overheard. "Telling the wife!" Mrs. Fettle called out scornfully. "Well, the wife's not having any, thank you, Joe Fettle."

"All right, all right. If you don't want to give us a hand, don't—"

"I'm going to do it," said Inga.

"Now, wait a minute," Joe began, dubiously.

"It's all fixed up," said his wife. "And what are you looking like that for? What's the matter with you, Joe? She'll be worth ten of that Daphne—"

"I never said she wouldn't, did I? Point is—it's illegal. She oughtn't to be mixed up in it. Wasn't even goin' to tell her where we'd gone to."

"I've told her already," said Mrs. Fettle. "So don't worry about that. I'm lending her a few things to-night and you're taking her up there when you take Alan. She wants to see her uncle. Then to-morrow I'll go and get her things from the people she's been staying with. That's so she won't be spotted and followed. We've worked it all out."

"You've been sharp about it—"

"We think fast, that's why. Don't we, duckie?"

"Yes, we do," said Inga. She went over to Alan, all dimples, sparkles, excitement. "This is going to be lovely fun, isn't it?"

"No," said Alan.

"I suppose you're sorry you can't take Daphne and that other woman with you, aren't you?"

"No," said Alan.

"Quite right. Then you're glad I'm coming?"

"No," said Alan. "I'm dead against it."

"Then don't speak to me again. I don't care what you think. I just want to see Uncle Roland and help him. And some of your beard's

113

coming off, just under your lower lip where you've spilt whisky on it."

An hour later, after being coldly ignored by Miss Dobb, Alan was trying to make himself comfortable on a camp-bed in a back room above the Metropolitan Dramatic and Music Academy. The room was bitterly cold and smelt of old magazines and mice. The camp-bed was too short for him, creakingly insecure, desperately uncomfortable. There were not enough bed-clothes. His beard worried him. He felt he ought to have had more whisky or less. No sweet and tender thoughts of the beautiful girl, no doubt already fast asleep two doors away down the corridor, visited him. A sniffling in the nose and a hot tickling sensation in the throat convinced him that he was about to develop a cold, which would probably be at its horrible height in two or three days, just about the time when Inspector Filer would place him under arrest. Not a promising outlook.

# CHAPTER VIII

# RATHER A FULL DAY

TWO DAYS later, towards the end of the morning, Alan was jotting down a charming little Rondo subject for the finale of his Suite. Dobb came charging in. Alan was annoyed, for although he had now a great affection for Dobb, he was anxious not to be interrupted. A man needed some time alone in his room.

"Where's Inga?" demanded Dobb.

"I don't know," said Alan.

"Why don't you know?"

"Because your niece and I haven't been on speaking terms since we arrived here, as you might have noticed. Just before we set out for this place, she asked me if I was glad she was coming too, and I told her I wasn't. I meant of course that I was sorry she wasn't keeping out of it, just as you were sorry—for her own sake. But she didn't take it in that sense. She has a gift of misinterpretation that almost amounts to genius. Is it a family trait, Dobb?"

"Certainly not." Dobb sat down on a box—for Alan's room could not be said to be furnished—relit his cigar and, to Alan's dismay, looked as if he were settling down for a long chat. "You ought to know by this time that most women haven't a glimmer of intuition. It's just what they lack. Everything's got to be made quite plain to them. A man never asks you what you're thinking or says, 'Tell me something', but women never stop. They just can't imagine what's going on in your mind. But I understood that you and Inga were in love with each other."

Alan frowned at him. "Have you a cigar with you? No? Well, that makes it all the worse. Now listen carefully, please. I sleep very badly here. I'm fighting a cold. We now have a lot of large fires up here, thanks to Joe's liberal supply of coal. But somebody has to bring up all that coal from the basement, and who's been doing it? Applerose—one of our more promising serious composers. That bent and blackened figure of toil you may have noticed, Dobb, is Applerose. Furthermore, this same Applerose, believe it or not, is beginning to feel rather bored with this radio programme that we've even started to rehearse, in our vanity and folly. He's all in favour of Dobb's Freedom Radio—or anybody's Freedom Radio—so long as he hasn't to take part in it or to listen to it. The truth about Applerose is—that unless his own compositions are being played, and well played too, he doesn't give a tinker's curse about radio—"

"And I'll tell *you* something now. Unless his inventions are being tried out, Dobb doesn't either. But what's all this to do with my niece?"

"You asked me if we were in love with one another. Now I expect that sort of thing from the Fettles, who are shameless sentimentalists, and, in between Black Market deals, live a sort of Christmas-card life. Moreover, twice, the entire staff of the Metropolitan Academy below—namely, Professor Wilfotstone and Miss Bunn—have asked me about Inga. And now, just when I have the chance of doing a little work, you of all men, Dobb, and at this time in the morning too, want to start one of those horribly intimate discussions of personal relationships that are difficult and embarrassing at any time. I agree, though, that Inga and I must settle something soon. We can't keep on hanging around each other and not being on speaking terms. There isn't any Norroland schnapps here yet, is there? I know Joe was trying to find some for us. It would help considerably. Incidentally, I'm getting tired of Beryl Fettle's ubiquitous frying-pan."

"I'm thinking of asking Professor Wilfotstone and Miss Bunn to a meal," said Dobb reflectively. "If I do, I'll cook it myself. But one of you will have to do my shopping. I ventured out yesterday afternoon—wearing the teeth and spectacles, of course—and took a taxi. The driver deliberately ignored a One Way Street sign, and when I told him he oughtn't to do that, do you know what he said? He gave me a wink and said, 'I'm a Dobbist. To hell with 'em. Ever listen to Dobb? That's the bloke for me.' Apparently there's a lot of that about. We aren't overdoing it, are we?"

"Probably. You're certainly overdoing it when you ask the Prof. and Miss Bunn to a meal." They were all that remained of the staff of the Metropolitan Dramatic and Music Academy, and were, Alan suspected, its proprietors. Miss Bunn, who was about seventy and rather small but somehow suggested Minor Royalty, taught music—

piano, violin (elementary), singing, the rudiments of harmony and counterpoint. Professor Wilfotstone was in charge of the Dramatic department, and looked like Henry Irving playing Liszt in his Abbé period; he had been a professional elocutionist, giving Dickens recitals in mechanics' institutes and temperance halls; and spoke with such strong consonants and pure vowel sounds that he seemed almost out of his mind. Inga and Mrs. Fettle adored him, chiefly because he took their fair white hands in his and complimented them, with grave nobility, on their Youthful Beauty and Exquisite Charm; but Alan kept well out of his way. "I'm against having them to a meal. Miss Bunn will fasten on to me—she knows I'm a musician—while the Prof. claims the attention of the Fair Sex, and you and Joe will be nicely out of it. I—"

Dobb stopped him, suddenly looking serious. "That could apply to other things too, Alan. Perhaps I've been a thoughtless, selfish old devil."

Alan stared at him. "What are you talking about?"

"You, chiefly. I've never given a thought to what all this nonsense,—first, the Dobbophone and Stannsen's symphony, then this Free Radio thing—might do to you. First, you lost your job with the E.B.C.—"

"My fault, not yours," said Alan quickly. "Besides, I was getting tired of them and their twilight melodies and features about Yugoslavia and their Fourth Programme unicorns. To say nothing of Lancelot and his Old Queen antics. No—no—"

"Now you're up to your neck in this Free Radio pickle," Dobb continued, ignoring Alan's protest. "I don't care a damn what happens to me, but you're young, a good composer, and with no money, I imagine—you haven't money, have you?"

"I've about two hundred and twenty pounds and a Steinway grand piano. Not much in some circles, in others almost a fortune. And stop apologizing. It doesn't sound right from you. And anyhow I've enjoyed myself, though I much preferred Joe Fettle's place, overheated and stuffy though it was, to this bleak Northern ruin—"

The door flew open. It was Inga, blazing with excitement. "Uncle Roland, come quickly. I've brought them back with me." She pulled him off the box and then began pushing him towards the door. When they reached it, she turned, somehow switched off her excitement in time to give Alan a cool disdainful look, and said with enormous condescension, "You can come too, if you wish. I don't suppose anybody'll mind."

"I mind," said Alan. "Kindly close the door." It banged.

He tried to develop the Rondo subject but nothing much came of it. Perhaps he no longer had any talent. As soon as he was through with this Dobbery, he decided, he would clear out of London, find some place out of the way and cheap to live in, and either write a big, solid work or pack it all up. One or the other. He worked out a few sketchy figures; he might get three hundred for his Steinway, pick up a decent little upright for fifty, that would leave him with two hundred and fifty—say he had four-fifty altogether, and then lived on five pounds a week—

Somebody was knocking on his door, in a gentlemanly but firm manner. Hoping that it had nothing to do with Inga's nonsense, about which he refused to be curious, he opened the door. There, an immense but noble ruin, was Professor Wilfotstone. "May I Trouble You for One Moment, my Dear Mr. Montgomery?" For Alan had retained the *alias* he had given Inspector Filer.

Once inside, almost filling the room, the Professor refused to occupy the solitary chair. "Still Roughing It, eh, my Dear Fellow? You Scientific Fellows seem quite indifferent to Creature Comforts—"

"Don't believe it," said Alan. "I think about nothing else. But what can I do for you, Professor Wilfotstone?"

"Just a Word of Advice," said the Professor, coming closer and smelling of cough mixture. He had eyes like an old lion; indeed, he was an old lion. "Your Chief has Very Kindly Invited Miss Bunn and Myself to dine with you all—to-morrow, I understand. Speaking for Miss Bunn as well as for Myself, I can say that the Invitation is Much Appreciated. And We Are Anxious—again I speak for Miss Bunn too—to Show Our Appreciation. Miss Bunn has a Little Recital all prepared, consisting, I gather of short pieces by Mendelssohn and Chaminade. Capital, capital—We All Agree. Now, as you know, Mr. Montgomery, before I retired from Recital Work I had a Large Repertoire of Carefully Selected Passages from our ever-beloved Charles Dickens. And this is the Question. Which, in Your View, would be preferred?"

"I really couldn't say," said Alan. "Wouldn't they be all rather long? We mustn't tire you."

"My *David Copperfield* might be Rather Exhausting, I Must

Confess, my Dear Fellow. *Pickwick* too is On The Long Side. My Own Preference is for *Dombey and Son*—with its Laughter, its Tears! Only this morning I recited a few sentences from the Death Of Little Paul to illustrate a point I was making. The student—a young policeman—"

"A policeman?" Alan was alarmed.

"It surprises you. He is on Night Duty this week—and gives up Part of his Well-earned Rest to attend my course. A Keen, Persevering Young Fellow, not without a Sense of the Dramatic, but still having Some Trouble with his O's and U's. I tell him," the Professor added, laughing heartily, "that if he will mind his O's and U's, I will mind my P's and Q's. Nothing like a Touch of Humour—"

The door had been left open, and now Inga marched in. "I'm sorry, Professor Wilfotstone—"

The Professor wheeled in a flash and at once had her hands in his and was bowing over them. "Capital, capital!" he boomed. "What A Pleasure indeed to see such Youth and Beauty! The Exquisite Lines of the Poet—"

"Dear Professor Wilfotstone, will you promise to recite them to me next time we meet? I have something rather urgent to say to Mr.—er—Montgomery—"

"Of course, of course—and I was About To Go. Capital, capital, capital!" And then the Professor was no longer with them.

Inga's line, new and unattractive, was indignant irony; and she started off on it at once. "Of course *you* wouldn't want to bother even coming as far as the next floor below, whoever was there, and of course after all its *only* the president of a country and *only* the greatest composer in the world—it's not as if it's anybody *important*—"

"What *is* all this? And stop talking in that silly way— or I'll shake you—"

"You daren't."

"All right, I daren't. But tell me properly or push off, Inga. I'm rather out of temper this morning. The coal-heaving on top of the bad nights and half a cold. Now then."

"Beryl lent me a veil, so I thought I'd risk going to the Norroland Embassy—"

"Did you clout anybody there, this time? My ear still sings."

"Serves you right for neglecting me the moment we were engaged. Anyhow, I went to the Embassy. And who did I find there?"

"This is like a cross-talk act. Who *did* you find there, Miss Dobb?"

"The President of Norroland, Dr. Bergenborg, who's an old sweetie-pie, and the great Stannsen—"

"Good God!" Alan hated to sound impressed, but there it was.

"You see," she cried triumphantly, as if some argument had been clinched. "They arrived last night—what's it—"

"What's what?"

"When nobody has to know who you are. Incognito, that's it. And now they're here."

"Do you mean here in this building?"

"I told you they were, only you wouldn't listen. They insisted on seeing Uncle Roland at once, so I brought them back with me, in an Embassy car, and we've brought a lot of Norroland things to eat—and a whole case of Norroland schnapps—"

"Let's go down. We're wasting time."

Alan looked at Stannsen first. Here, in a world of robots, sheep, monkeys and rats, was a Man. He was rather shorter than Alan had imagined him to be, but tremendously broad and massive; he was so bald and brown that he might have been a highly polished wood-carving of himself; his eyes were small and deep-set but sparkled and glittered in their caverns like Peruvian diamonds; his manner was large and genial, his voice loud and careless, his English murderous; and Alan loved him at first sight. When Inga introduced him, Stannsen gave him a sharp look, then crowned his day by telling him that he remembered hearing his piano quartet broadcast from London a year ago. To prove it, Stannsen, who obviously had an astounding musical memory, described the work in some detail, with some assistance from Inga, as an interpreter.

The President of Norroland was a tall, bulky man with a long nose and forked grey beard, not unlike a sorcerer in a Russian opera. Clearly he was enjoying himself away from politics and solemn occasions. He and Stannsen and Dobb were already drinking Norroland schnapps, and Alan made haste to join them. Inga went off to help Mrs. Fettle with lunch. Joe was out somewhere. Dobb and Stannsen now began arguing in Norrolandish, with occasional interruptions by Dr. Bergenborg, who had Hafstalman's trick of suddenly bellowing with laughter. As *Strunshka* and *dumkas* were frequently mentioned, and there were some references to the Dobbophone, Alan knew what they were talking about—the famous game over which they had quarrelled. Down went the schnapps, up went their voices; and Dr.

Bergenborg slapped his knee harder and harder and laughed longer and longer. Inga returned to announce that lunch was ready.

"They really are ridiculous," she told Alan. "Like two great babies. What do you think they're going to do after lunch?"

"My guess is—play another game of *Strunshka*," said Alan promptly. "With the President as referee."

"No, he's going to play too. He's as bad as they are, except that he knows it's silly. And they're going to play for fifteen thousand *dumkas*—those are points—so that it'll take hours and hours and hours. It's going to be *Strunshka* and schnapps now for the rest of the day. Idiots."

"Probably they'll end up in *Schnapps-sunlight*—"

"Now don't you start that nonsense again." But there was no time for more warnings. They were at the lunch table, rich and strange with Norroland delicacies. Alan could feel the schnapps at work already; the first floor of the Metropolitan Academy was not its usual decayed and depressing self; there were hints already of a mysterious sunlight and Northern sorcery.

"Inga, it is a good younger, I think," roared Stannsen, pointing at Alan. "He makes the love good, eh? But as—as—what am I with you in English?"

"Godfather," said Inga, who ought to have been blushing but wasn't.

"Godfather. As godfather I say I do not like the beard. It is not a good beard. I say he cannot marry you with such a beard."

"It isn't his beard," cried Inga. "He put it on as a disguise. And now it's coming to pieces. You'll have to do something about it, Alan darling."

This disguise business had then to be explained to Stannsen and Dr. Bergenborg, who roared with laughter. Alan decided that after lunch he would remove the beard, disguise or no disguise, for it really was moulting badly. Partly in English, partly in Norrolandish, Dobb told them about his Freedom Radio. The Norroland papers had carried the story, but the President had been too busy with other things to bother about it, and Stannsen, it appeared, never read newspapers. What had brought them over was the question of the Stannsen concert. After he had been told of Alan's connection with the E.B.C., Dr. Bergenborg, serious for once, asked him to explain what had happened and then told him why this was not entirely a laughing matter.

"We are very proud of Stannsen in Norroland, Mr. Applerose," he said. "We put him in our window for the world to admire. Now we need more trade with Britain. I am here to discuss that, if possible to sign an agreement. We want the British to remember us in Norroland. So we ask Stannsen as a good patriot to offer London his new symphony. He does so, but, as you see, he is a humorous man and he makes this condition of the Dobbophone. It is nonsense, a joke between old friends. But then there is much publicity, not only in Britain and in Norroland but everywhere in Europe, even in America, about this Dobbophone. There are too many jokes for some of our people at home. My political opponents make use of these jokes. Norroland, they say, is being made to look foolish. What should have been good for our British relations is now not so good, perhaps quite bad. That is why we come quietly, incognito, to try and settle this thing. If it can be settled by more *Strunshka,* all in secret, then let us have more *Strunshka.* I will play too because I am a better player than either of them. And know all the rules." Now he roared with laughter again.

Apparently it was impossible to have any kind of Norroland lunch without toasts being drunk. Now they were at it again; and Alan felt that if he were not careful he would be kissing Inga in public again and once more find himself faced with the Betrothal Bumper. So he ate a great deal, though not as much as Stannsen and Dr. Bergenborg, who were giant trenchermen.

"Where's Joe?" he asked Mrs. Fettle. He was giving her a hand clearing some dishes, for Inga was listening to Dr. Bergenborg.

"Out on some business. I hope he'll be back soon and not miss these two. Just fancy—a President! And so nice and affable. And Mr. Stannsen—of course I've often seen *his* photo too. My goodness—can't they put it away? That's what I like to see—men like that, really tucking in. Does your heart good to see 'em. And laugh. That's how men ought to be, I say. And half the time, when you see women looking so miserable nowadays, it's 'cos men aren't like that any more. I'll bet that Mr. Stannsen's been a wicked lad in his time." She almost smacked her lips over the thought of his wickedness. Then she gave him a look, essentially and deeply feminine. "It's about time you got on with something, isn't it? A girl like that, and you don't seem to know how to start." And this, together with the schnapps, was not without its influence on the events of the afternoon.

Towards the end of lunch, Stannsen, now enormously expansive, began to talk to Alan about music, after first expressing his doubts about Sir Lancelot Telly. "Making music comes from mind—from heart—from nerves. All is good. Too much of one is not good. Now is nearly all nerves. It is music of dislike and fear. Sometimes too much mind—very cold—classical—dull. It is so with you perhaps. Do you live rich life?"

"No, he doesn't," said Inga. "Even though he had two girls draped round him the other night."

"Hold tongue, Inga," roared Stannsen. "We talk of music—art—man's life."

"My work's been on the dull side," Alan confessed. "I try to get far away from my film and radio stuff, the vulgar style, and then I suppose I become too cool and fastidious. This idea of highbrow music and lowbrow music in opposition hasn't been good for us, I'm certain."

"So am I certain. I was lucky to be mostly before this time and in a small country. So I try to make music best I know, with mind, with heart, with nerves, out of love of country and people and rich life of man. Not rich money life but life rich in feeling." Stannsen smiled reminiscently. "I have good rich life."

"You're a wicked old man," said Inga.

"Artist must be wicked old man too. Must know and feel shadow life. Hell and Heaven—both must be there. Dobb, my friend," he shouted, "you pretend to forget we play *Strunshka*. You are afraid to be beaten again. You cannot play *Strunshka*—you cannot even play Dobbophone—you cannot play any things—"

"You beat me fairly and squarely at *Strunshka*" cried Dobb, already high-coloured and perhaps touched with *Schnapps-sunlight*, "and I'll play a Dobbophone solo for you if you insist on it. Let's make a start. What about cards?"

"O-ho, I have them with me," said Stannsen. "New cards. So you do not say I cheat you if I win."

"We play for fifteen thousand *dumkas*," said Dobb, rising. "I doubt if Bergenborg is in our class at all—"

"I am the second best *Strunshka* player in the whole world," said Dr. Bergenborg firmly. "And the best is certainly not here. He is old Drend, the secretary of the Baltic Union Club—"

"Nonsense," said Dobb. "Now let us understand one another. We ignore Bergenborg's score, Stannsen. That's agreed. He's in with us just to see how the game ought to be played by first-rate men. If you score more *dumkas* than I do, then I play my Dobbophone for you. If I win, you make me a public apology. Agreed?"

*"D'accord."* Stannsen took his coat off. "Inga, please bring glasses, plenty of Norroland schnapps, and a little water. And we must have quietness so that Dr. Bergenborg and your Uncle Roland can think hard about the game. It will last a very long time."

Alan helped the women to clear the lunch table while the three formidable elderly men, all now in their shirt-sleeves and smoking large cigars, took their places for the game. Then he assisted at the washing-up, feeling, if truth be told, rather out of it and somewhat emasculated, as he heard the distant roars of the gaming males. He had been careful not to drink much schnapps at lunch, and now began to wonder if he had not been too careful. Mrs. Fettle announced that she was going to lie down. Inga said she would retire too. She gave Alan a sidelong look that meant something, though he was not sure what that something was. "You'd better go and lie down too, hadn't you?" she said. "Or write some music."

He walked off. He went to have a look at the card-players, now triumphantly banging down their kings and aces in an atmosphere thick with smoke and reeking of schnapps. He found a glass and helped himself. The little torchlight procession began. Strange thoughts, noble ideas, sprang out of the dead ground of the afternoon. After several glasses, the torches were larger and brighter and a band or two accompanied the procession. The three at the table began to look like majestic archetypes. Even the *Strunshka* they played so noisily, with much ungentlemanly boasting and jeering, was almost something in a saga. Alan's heart went out to Norroland. Although he had never been there, it was now his favourite country. He drank to it, spilled some schnapps, and in drying his chin found that he had removed half his beard. In the large ruin of a bathroom, which had the atmosphere and many of the sounds of a ship's engine-room but hardly ever any hot water, he removed what remained of the beard. This was achieved not without difficulty and pain, especially as he felt he ought to shave once all the crepe hair had gone; but it was difficulty and pain operating at a far remove, below the horizon, well out of reach of his central being; for now he was moving again in *Schnapps-sunlight*. He floated upstairs, along a landing, knocked at a door and behind it discovered Miss Inga Dobb wearing a blue dressing-gown, polishing her nails, and looking very bored.

"The question is," he began at once, ignoring some feeble protest she appeared to be making, "how can I express—immediately, without the least delay—my appreciation of, my devotion to, this astonishing country of Norroland. The slightest interruption of the *Strunshka* game, I felt, wouldn't be welcome, however eloquent my tribute might be. But then I said to myself, 'Miss Dobb is here. Miss Dobb who—'"

"Seeing that you've barged in here without being asked," said Miss Dobb, "you might as well call me Inga—"

"But I said to myself, 'Inga is here, young and fair and blooming. Inga, in whose eyes Norroland—"

"Norroland what?"

"I've forgotten that part. A man can't remember everything. What I ask myself—and only the speakers on the E.B.C. Fourth Programme ask themselves more questions than I do—what I ask myself is this. Do I worship Inga because she is a symbol of Norroland? Or do I love Norroland because it has given me you, Inga?"

"It hasn't given you me. And you've been drinking schnapps again, haven't you?"

"Possibly. But these sentiments don't come from the schnapps. The schnapps merely remove certain inhibitions, thereby enabling me to express the sentiments."

"If you love me, say so." Inga sat up, bright and expectant.

"Certainly." He plucked her out of the chair, gathered her in his arms, kissed her mouth, her right eyelid, her left eyelid, the end of her nose, then her lips again.

"Darling," cried Inga.

Now he sat on the chair himself but pulled Inga down with him, giving her barely time to adjust herself so that she could struggle without anything coming of it.

"We're too apt to talk," said Alan, "as if thoughts and feelings could be found in substances themselves. But clearly they're in ourselves, and the substances merely help us to discover them."

"Darling," cried Inga.

"If, for example, I'm highly metaphysical when under the influence of nitrous oxide gas at the dentist's—as I usually am—this doesn't mean that the metaphysics are in the gas but are in me."

"What's this got to do with us?" said Inga.

"They prove my point about the schnapps. The sentiments are in me, not in the schnapps, which, I repeat, merely removes certain inhibitions."

"But does this mean that every time I want you to make love to me I'll have to give you a lot of schnapps?"

"No, probably the inhibitions will begin to remove themselves. Which opens a much larger question—"

"Is it about us?"

"No. Except as members of the human race—"

"Darling, have we to bother about the whole human race?"

"If chemical changes can remove inhibitions, which in turn—"

"Kiss me."

He kissed the right side of her neck, the lobe of her right ear, the delicious fat bit over her cheek-bone, the right corner of her mouth; and then she took charge herself, with the result that nothing was said for about ten minutes.

"Darling, darling," cried Inga, pulling herself back a little to see him better, as if he had just been awarded to her as a prize.

"As I was saying, if chemical changes can remove inhibitions, which in turn enable us to—"

"When shall we get married, darling?"

"Don't let's bother."

"Oh—darling! Do you mean you just want to live with me? Or perhaps you don't even want that—only to pop in on Tuesdays."

"Certainly not. But this engagement business frightens me, my beautiful golden rabbit—"

"Why am I your beautiful golden rabbit?"

"I haven't the least idea. But I say this engagement business frightens me. I'll find myself downing another colossal Norroland Betrothal Bumper, then doing something wrong, then back again to the Embassy, with Dr. Trock called in for the Breaking Ceremony. You'll give me another fearful clout, I'll swallow the Breaking Bumper in one, and probably this time I'll go berserk, knock Trock for six, and be laid out for a week by Hafstalman, who must weigh about nineteen stone."

"But you can't behave like this with me, darling, unless we're engaged."

"Yes, I can." And he did, without much further talk, while dusk crept into the Finsbury Park area, the firelight flickered round the room, and somewhere not far away the traffic of the rush hour hooted and groaned.

Finally, Inga said, "We'll just be engaged in the English way, then. How will that do, darling?"

"Very nicely, my pet. So long as we don't tell anybody and I haven't to buy a ring. No, no—I don't mean it. We'll have an English engagement, then a Norroland marriage, with special old schnapps by the gallon and Vikings holding crossed whale-bones outside the church. Have you any money, by the way, Inga?"

"No, darling. You have some, haven't you?"

"Not much. I've been thinking about it. Come here." She twined herself about him, and for the next half-hour they talked about money, trying to decide whether the Steinway ought to be sacrificed. When they had done, Alan said, "Well, that's the only talk about money I ever enjoyed. We must talk a lot about money, Inga."

"Let's go down and tell everybody now," said Inga. "Wait outside a minute, darling."

In an atmosphere thicker than ever, the *Strunshka* match was still being played. Alan helped himself to schnapps. Inga announced in her loudest voice that she and Alan were now really engaged and hoped to marry shortly. The three old monsters merely looked up for a second, nodded vaguely, then continued playing. Feeling that she could not have been heard properly, Inga tried again, with the same result.

"You're disgusting," she told them. "I'll go and tell Mrs. Fettle. And Alan—if you ever start playing this wretched game, I'll never speak to you again." And off she went.

Dobb looked up. "It's a foolish game—but now you'd better learn to play it, as a matter of principle. Don't stand that nonsense from Inga, or you'll never be able to call your soul your own."

"I'll think that over. How many *dumkas* have you scored, Dobb?"

"Twelve thousand six hundred and eighty-five. I'm rather behind. Out of practice, of course. I wonder if Joe has any beer. You might go and see."

Joe was in the kitchen with Inga and Mrs. Fettle, who were standing close together, babbling about the engagement. Joe shook hands and congratulated Alan. "Knew it from the start, Alan boy. As the wife has always said—you were the Only One. How's it going along there? Dobb's behind, isn't he? I'll offer you eight to five against Dobb comin' in second, eleven to five he doesn't win. An' don't think Dobb's radio'll get goin' to-night. Look at the time already. Any bets on the game?"

"What are you offering for the President?"

"Even money. You can have five to three against Stannsen."

"The President to win—two pounds. What about this beer?"

"Beryl ducks," cried Joe, "get some sandwiches an' cold stuff ready—we'll take 'em in with the beer. Now let me see if I've got these bets right."

It was nearly nine o'clock when the great game ended. The last half-hour, when Inga and Alan and the Fettles watched every card, was tremendously exciting. It opened with a remarkable spurt from Dobb, who for a few minutes was actually leading and at once was hoarsely and insufferably triumphant. But then the President, the coolest of the three and the man for Alan's money, began quietly piling *dumkas* without looking as if he were making much progress, thanks to his political training. Stannsen, looking by this time rather like an active volcano, banged down more and more kings and aces, and went jeering and crowing on his way to victory. In the end, Dobb, now a purple wet ruin, was left behind; it was neck and neck between the Norrolanders; then the President just scraped home with a sixty-five *dumka* lead. Hands were shaken, backs slapped, toasts drunk; Mrs. Fettle was hugged by Stannsen, Inga's left cheek tickled by the President's beard.

"Very well, I admit it," said Dobb. "Owing to lack of practice, I was beaten. By both of you. And I'm a man of my word. I said I'd play my Dobbophone, and now I'm ready to play it whenever and wherever you please, Stannsen. In fact, just to prove that I'm all set to keep my word, I'll play it *now*."

"Oh—no, Uncle, *please!*" cried Inga. "Let's enjoy ourselves."

"I propose," said Dobb, with a solemnity that suggested *Schnapps-sunlight* to Alan, "to add to your enjoyment." He made a move towards the door.

But the door opened before he could reach it. The man who came in was a dark, foxy sort of chap in a mackintosh, and before anybody could ask him what he wanted, he told them they could all consider themselves under arrest.

"And who the blazes are you?" demanded Dobb.

"Sutcliff's the name. Detective-sergeant. You're Dobb, aren't you? Well, just keep back. I'll sort out the rest of you in a minute. And if anybody's got any funny ideas, I'd like to point out that I'm considered fairly tough and that I've five men with me, all on the hefty side."

"Why don't you call out the Grenadier Guards?" said Fettle.

Mrs. Fettle came forward, bristling. "Don't be silly," she told the sergeant. "Coming in talking like that! Good gracious!"

"I'm not concerned with you ladies," said the sergeant. "If you'd like to withdraw, you can. But if you stay, kindly keep quiet." He looked at Alan, who was nearer to him than Dr. Bergenborg and Stannsen were. "What's your name?"

"Bernard Montgomery," said Alan promptly. "No relation of the Field-Marshal. Just a coincidence—"

"That'll do," said the sergeant sourly. "You're Applerose. We know about you." He went forward. "Now what about you two?"

"I'm Dr. Bergenborg—the President of Norroland—"

"That's right," said the sergeant wearily, "and I'm General Franco. Now turn it up, will you? We're not at the Victoria Palace. And I'm not in the mood," he added, shouting now. "I ought to be off duty by this time."

"If you're not careful, chum," said Fettle, "you'll soon be off duty for the rest of your natural."

"Hello—another of 'em," the sergeant began, still shouting.

But then Inspector Filer arrived. His face seemed larger and meatier than ever, his features smaller; it was like a squirrel looking out of a side of beef. He was very pleased with himself, clapped his enormous hands together and then rubbed them hard. "Well, well, well, well, well—quite a party!"

"It's Dobb and Applerose all right, sir," said the sergeant. "But I don't know yet about these others. Just had some sauce from that one—wouldn't give his name."

Inspector Filer stared aggressively at Dr. Bergenborg. "Looks to me uncommonly like old Ike Shultz, the con man who used to ride the tubs to New York. How are you these days, Ike?"

"You are an imbecile," said Dr. Bergenborg. Stannsen roared with laughter.

"I've seen that one before too," said the sergeant.

"Some of the old ones are the worst," said Inspector Filer. "You'd think they'd learn more sense." He turned to Joe. "Who are you?"

"Fettle's the name—Joe Fettle."

"I've heard about you. Union Jack Novelty Company—eh? One of the fly boys. Well, pleased to meet you."

"Can't say the same," said Joe. "But no rudeness intended. I'll tell you chaps straight—you're runnin' bang into big trouble. This gentleman really *is* the President of Norroland—"

"Of course he is," said Inspector Filer. "That's why he comes up here to play a nice game of cards. Next week you're having the King of Sweden and the Pope." He looked at the sergeant. "Why do they do it? What do they think we are? Oh dear, dear, dear!" The inspector shut his eyes and wagged his head.

At this moment Miss Helen Mick came rushing in. "Good evening. Good evening. Applerose, how's your love life?"

"We're engaged," said Inga hastily.

"Now, Miss Mick," said Inspector Filer, "you've no business in here. I'm not ready to make a statement to the press yet, though when I am you won't be disappointed—it looks like being very juicy. We've got all sorts up here."

But Miss Mick was not listening to him: she was staring hard at Stannsen and Dr. Bergenborg. Then she turned to Alan. "What's going on here, Applerose?"

"You'd better ask the inspector. He knows."

"But if that's not the great Stannsen, then it's his double." She had another look at him.

"Stannsen—yes." And Stannsen gave her an enormous wink. "You look at me. I look at you. Better for me. Preddy eyes—preddy girl. You come here—we talk."

"Now, behave yourself," said Inga severely. "Besides, you must be careful—she's a journalist—on the *Morning Star.*"

"You shut up and look after Applerose," said Miss Mick. "Golly—the great Stannsen. And what a man too!" She drifted closer.

"You like me. I like you." Stannsen beamed at her. "Now you meet my friend, Dr. Bergenborg—"

"We do not talk with the press, please, Stannsen," said Dr. Bergenborg sharply.

"Of course," cried Miss Mick. "And I know who you are too, now."

"What *is* all this?" said the inspector.

Then Sir Lancelot Telly walked in. He was wearing an extra-large black-and-white check coat, a lilac-coloured waistcoat with silver buttons, and some sort of pale yellow silk stock; and he made a magnificent entrance. Ignoring everybody else he waddled up to Stannsen. "My dear Stannsen, allow me to welcome you to London—to tell you how delighted we all are to know you're here. I heard a rumour this morning, went along to your Embassy early this evening, and was fortunate enough to find the chauffeur who'd brought you up here. Your symphony's a great work—and for me and my orchestra a great privilege—a great pleasure—"

"Thank you," said Stannsen with dignity. "Mr. President—this is the conductor of the E.B.C. Symphony Orchestra—Sir Lancelot Telly."

"Mr. President," cried Sir Lancelot, already seeing the Order of Noble Norsemen glittering on his dress shirt-front, "what a privilege—what an honour!"

"My God! " cried Miss Mick. "If anybody tries to stop me writing about this, I'll kill him."

Sir Lancelot now noticed Alan. "Alan, my dear boy, how are you?"

"I'm well, Lancelot, but about to be arrested. And so is Mr. Dobb there. By the way, you'll be relieved to know he's agreed to play his Dobbophone now. It's all settled."

"Splendid, splendid!" Sir Lancelot insisted upon shaking hands with Dobb.

Inspector Filer coughed. Everybody looked at him: it was that kind of cough. "I recognize you, of course, Sir Lancelot—"

"I'm delighted to hear it. Ought I to recognize you?"

"No, sir. Filer's the name. Inspector. And I must explain to you—and to these—er—foreign gentlemen—that I have definite instructions to take Mr. Dobb and Mr. Applerose into custody."

"Quite, quite. This pirate radio thing, of course. Mr. Dobb—Alan—you really were very naughty, you know—everybody's furious. The Air Marshal's been almost out of his mind, if he can be said to have a mind. And the Government are very angry, I know for a fact. My cousin Margery, a tiresome girl—married a politician, Sir Wilfred Gallater, who's now Home Secretary or whatever he's called—and she told me that he and his friends are all absolutely *livid*. Now what can we do about this? No, Inspector, not that cough again, *please*. We must think."

"It's out of this world," said Miss Mick dreamily. "I knew, if I was a good girl, something like this might happen."

"Oh—you are good girl," said Stannsen, twinkling at her. "Is a pity."

"I'm not *that* good, don't worry. Golly—what a personality!" She sat on the arm of his chair.

Dr. Bergenborg, very much the President, now took charge. "Inspector, you have some cars here?"

"Yes, sir, two."

"Then you must take us to the Norroland Embassy. You have my personal guarantee that Mr. Dobb and Mr. Applerose will not run away. We can all do more there than we can here. And there is much to be done. You agree to this? Good. I am sorry I called you an imbecile. Let us go."

Dr. Bergenborg, Stannsen, Miss Mick and Sir Lancelot rode in one car; Alan and Inga and Dobb, with Inspector Filer, in the other. The Fettles were left behind as the police had no charge against them. At the Embassy, Stannsen disappeared, with Miss Mick still in attendance; Dr. Bergenborg vanished into the Ambassador's room, to send some messages; Sir Lancelot went off to get into touch with his cousin, Lady Gallater; and Alan, Inga, Dobb and Inspector Filer were taken up to the room where the Breaking Ceremony had taken place, and where, a little later, they were joined by Hafstalman, who immediately produced some schnapps. The inspector was called away to speak to Scotland Yard.

"Now perhaps we drink again the Betrothal Bumper," said Hafstalman.

"No," said Inga.

"I'm afraid not," said Alan. "I'm a fair way towards *Schnapps-sunlight* now, and that Betrothal Bumper might lay me out. Though of course, if I'm to be arrested and carted off to gaol, I might as well be out."

"Darling," cried Inga, "if you go to prison, then I shall go too."

"Not allowed," said Alan. "They wouldn't feel they were punishing a man if they let a wench like you share his cell."

"Thank you, darling. But I can't believe it'll happen. Uncle, what do *you* think?"

"I don't know," said Dobb, who looked to Alan as if he were now in full *Schnapps-sunlight*. "Strictly speaking, I've stopped thinking. I stopped just after lunch, when we began that infernal *Strunshka*. But

I've had my fun, and now I'm ready to pay for it."

"So am I," said Alan, "if the worst comes to the worst. But I'd rather it didn't."

"I shall tell them," said Dobb, "that I coerced you into helping me."

"You will not," said Alan. "And if you did, they wouldn't believe you. Hafstalman, I wish you'd go down and see what's happening. You could go with him, Inga."

Left to themselves, the two criminals had two more glasses of schnapps each, muttered a little, then fell asleep. Alan found himself embarking for some mysterious voyage on a ship that was about half a mile long and only ten feet broad; it seemed to take him several dream hours to find his cabin, which he was sharing with Bernard Shutmill, Dr. Grenf (the Central European correspondent), and Alfred and Louis Sauvager of Clermont-Ferrand. The cabin was very crowded at first but then began elongating itself, until finally an officious type of chap brought in three horses. "I'm taking them out at Milan," he explained. "They're Wednesday-Thursday horses with eight stars." Then Alan, baffled, woke up.

Inga was back, and with her were Stannsen and Miss Mick. "Are you all right, darling?" asked Inga.

"No. I had an idiotic dream, and now when I get out of it I find myself here, waiting to be arrested again by Inspector Filer or to be pardoned by Lancelot's cousin's husband, all of which is nearly as idiotic. I'm also very hungry."

"So am I, darling," said Inga. "After all, it's about eleven o'clock and we've had no dinner, only a couple of sandwiches. I don't think you ought to have any more schnapps, darling."

"I must have something," said Alan, helping himself.

"We ah have more schnapps," said Stannsen.

"Certainly," said Dobb, waking at that very moment. "What's happening about this police business?"

"Miss Mick, you explain," said Inga.

"Everybody's been telephoning like mad," said Miss Mick, accepting a glass of schnapps from Stannsen. "High-level stuff. Now there's a little conference assembling below—Public Prosecutor, Commissioner of Police, and so forth—and they're waiting for Sir Wilfred Gallater. As soon as he's here, they'll probably send for you two—"

"And, Uncle Roland, please," cried Inga, "you must be nice to them."

"Why?" asked Dobb, who certainly did not look as if he were ready to be nice to anybody.

"You know jolly well why. And you too, Alan darling. Otherwise they'll send you to prison."

"Is too foolish," said Stannsen. "They make themselves fools. Miss Mick, who is clever girl, say this also."

"All I ask," said Miss Mick, "is just a chance to tell them so. I want to give them the press angle. I've done some ringing up too."

Hafstalman and Inspector Filer now arrived, to say that Dobb and Alan were wanted below. The others insisted upon accompanying them. They all sat in a little ante-room, staring at the door behind which the high-level types were now in session. Then Inspector Filer took Dobb inside, and returned to guard the door. He told Alan that his turn would come shortly, so Alan stood just behind the door, hoping to overhear at least some of Dobb's remarks.

Somebody in there must have suggested to Dobb that he should regard the proceedings as being strictly confidential. Alan caught most of his reply. "It depends what comes of these proceedings," Dobb told them. "If I'm to be regarded as a member of the criminal classes, I shall behave like one." Then a lot of inaudible stuff from the other people, to which Dobb replied, "If you want to prefer serious charges, go ahead. I'm not asking for any favours. I've been telling people that nowadays we're overgoverned to the point of tyranny. If you think that putting me in the dock will prove I'm wrong, go ahead and try it."

Inga joined Alan at the door. "Do you think Uncle Roland is making a good impression, darling?"

"It depends what you mean by a good impression," said Alan.

"Oh—dear—he's being rude to them, isn't he?"

There was more blah-blah. Then an angrier voice could be heard, asking Dobb if it was necessary to take that tone, as some of them didn't like it.

"Possibly, possibly," they heard Dobb roar. "But I'm not trying to find the tone you like. You're assuming now that you're more important than I am. And I don't think you are. No doubt I couldn't do your jobs, whatever they are, but I'm damned certain you couldn't do mine. The increasing self-importance of you fellows is one of the things I dislike—"

"Oh dear—oh dear!" cried Inga.

The door flew open. Dobb, bristling, scarlet, blazing-eyed, came marching out. "Hope you'll do better with those fellows than I did, Alan." And he went to join Stannsen, who immediately roared with laughter at the very sight of him.

"Darling, darling, do be calm and nice," cried Inga, as Inspector Filer beckoned him through the doorway. Seated in a semi-circle were half a dozen high-level personages, looking very important, very grave, and rather overdoing it like small-part players in a film. The two most important seemed to be a pale, eggy man, wearing two pairs of spectacles, and a beaky legal-eagle type, to whom Alan took an instant dislike.

"Mr. Applerose," said eggy double-spectacles, "sit down, please. And no speeches, if you don't mind. We haven't much time. As usual, the press are on our heels. Sir Thomas?"

The beaky legal-eagle nodded, then looked severely at Alan. "I shall put some questions to you, and I suggest that you confine yourself to a plain *Yes* or *No*."

"Well, I'm against it," said Alan, who suddenly felt quite at ease. He looked at the others. "I'm sorry, gentlemen, but I've always felt this *Yes or No* technique to be a fraud. And as this isn't a court of law, I don't see why I should be tricked into it."

"Come—come—" beaky Sir Thomas began, scowling hard.

But a smallish man, with a humorous face, intervened. "Mr. Chairman, I'm inclined to agree with Mr. Applerose. I suggest that you, sir, ask him a few questions and let him answer them in his own way."

"Very well," said eggy double-spectacles, the Chairman. "I should like you to tell us something about Dobb, who seems to have been—er—dining and not disposed to explain himself properly. What were his motives in attempting to run this radio programme?"

"I think I understand them all right, Mr. Chairman," said Alan, smiling. "Dobb's an inventor—and quite a good one, I imagine. So he wanted to try out a new transmitter he'd invented—very powerful over a short range, and very compact."

"That sounds a fair description, sir," said the man with the humorous face, probably a technical type. "And I must say I'd like to have a look at it. Sorry, Mr. Applerose. Go on."

"Dobb also wanted to let some steam off, and, what with one

135

thing and another, you can't blame him—"

"Come, come now," said beaky Sir Thomas, scowling again. "If we all began running radio programmes just because we wanted to let steam off, as you call it, what would happen? Tell me that."

"You know," said Alan easily, "I've never thought much of that *if-we-all-did-it* argument. It sounds reasonable, but it isn't. We couldn't all invent a new transmitter, could we? Dobb's an exceptional man, that's the answer. And perhaps exceptional men have to let steam off. Finally, Dobb wanted to prove that a man could run his own radio programme if he chose to. So he did it."

"And broke the law," said one of them.

"Yes," said Alan. "And I broke it with him."

"And what was *your* motive?" asked the Chairman, taking off one pair of spectacles. "Money? Notoriety? What?"

"I received no money for myself," said Alan. "And, believe it or not, I detest notoriety. I did it chiefly because I liked Dobb and was irritated and bored by the E.B.C., from which I resigned. If I'd thought Dobb could do any real harm, I wouldn't have helped him. But I felt— and still feel—he did more good than harm. And anyhow it's all over now."

"Because the police finally put their hands on you," said Sir Thomas severely.

"No, it was finished anyhow. We'd packed up to-night's show before the police arrived. Dobb was too busy finishing a card game. However, if you haul us into court, it won't be finished. Then the fun will really begin. With clever counsel to defend us, and half the press of Europe reporting the case, mostly in our favour, you'll have something much worse than a little pirate radio programme on your hands. In my opinion, you'll be made to look either vindictive or foolish. Just out there, dying to talk to you, gentlemen, is a Miss Helen Mick of the *Morning Star*. Why not have her in, to tell you what the press thinks?"

They looked at one another and then there was some discussion. Beaky Tom was dead against it, and carried two others with him, but the other three, including the Chairman, were in favour of hearing Miss Mick, who was finally ushered in by Inspector Filer.

"Yes, Applerose is quite right," she cried, after the Chairman had put a question to her. "Half a dozen of us, all with by-lines in the big dailies, know what's happening here. And I might as well tell you—if you go for these two, we're going for you—that's settled already. Dobb's been good value to us—we like him—and so do a lot of our readers—and if you put him and Applerose through your legal sausage machine, there'll be a hell of a rumpus. People are bored—you must know that—and they're just waiting for something like this. And—oh boy—what we'll do with it!"

"Really, Mr. Chairman," said beaky Tom, scowling harder than ever, "I must protest against this. We're not to be intimidated in this fashion. I suggest the Law should take its course—"

"One moment, Sir Thomas. Yes, Miss Mick?"

"You can do more harm to yourselves in five minutes than Dobb could do in five years," said Miss Mick earnestly. "Take that high stuffy line—and most of you have had it. You'll be out."

She stopped there because now Dr. Bergenborg came in, with a word of apology to the Chairman, who assured him respectfully that his presence was most welcome. Dr. Bergenborg sat down, looking very impressive, and smilingly indicated to Miss Mick that she must continue.

"I'll just say this," said Miss Mick. "If I had this little problem dumped into my lap, I know what I'd do. First, I'd call off all the legal bloodhounds, and stop the sausage machine. Next, I'd save my face by announcing that really I'd been in this all the time, trying out Dobb's transmitter and testing public opinion on independent radio. Then nobody could laugh at me. Well, I'll wait outside until you're ready to give me the story. Chin up, Applerose!" And she gave him a grin, then hurried out.

Everybody began talking at once but Dr. Bergenborg soon made himself heard above the rest, and after a few moments he was given respectful attention. "Thank you, gentlemen. I realize of course that I have no place in these proceedings, that it is only by an accident that I am here. But I have been speaking to your Foreign Secretary, who asked me to give you my opinion. Perhaps it may be of interest if I tell you how it seems to a friendly foreign observer who is not without political experience. Do you agree?"

"We welcome it, Mr. President," said the Chairman, taking off his last pair of spectacles and almost changing into somebody else.

"Thank you," said Dr. Bergenborg, looking larger and more formidable than ever. "Now, gentlemen: of the Great Powers, Britain is no longer the richest and strongest. But we still look to her for something that is very rare among the rich and powerful — for a spirit of humour, a spirit of tolerance. Very precious indeed in this iron world, gentlemen. There was much talk just after the War of a Third Force, you will remember. But the real Third Force is this spirit of humour, of tolerance, of a liberal humanism that does not take itself too seriously."

There were murmurs of agreement from most of them, a notable exception being beaky, black-browed Sir Thomas, who was probably longing for birch rods, whips, irons and gibbets.

"I am sorry to say, gentlemen," Dr. Bergenborg continued, "that some of us observe signs that your country is in danger of losing this spirit. If you lost it altogether, that would be a grave defeat for civilised humanity. Now, I feel that in this matter of Mr. Dobb — and, as you know, we in Norroland are interested too — you have an opportunity to prove your doubting critics right or wrong. If the world laughs *with* you, all will be well. If the world laughs *at* you, it will already feel that it has more humour, more tolerance, a more liberal spirit, than you have. That young woman showed you, with true feminine cunning, a way out. I advise you to take it."

"Mr. Chairman," said beaky Tom with harsh emphasis, "with all due respect to our distinguished visitor, I think he can hardly demand that we should halt the processes of our Law — "

"Sir, I made no such demand," said Dr. Bergenborg. "I merely suggested that a spirit of humorous tolerance might be displayed. But I will make a further point, gentlemen. Dobb came into prominence first, as you may remember, through his association with our great Norroland composer, Stannsen. If Dobb is not free to play in Stannsen's symphony, Stannsen will not allow the work to be performed. The concert, partly in honour of my visit, will then be cancelled. Political considerations, gentlemen, may then compel me to cancel that visit — for as yet, you understand, I am here unofficially. As I told you, your Foreign Secretary and I have already had some talk on this subject. He asked me to give you my views. That is all. Thank you, gentlemen. Mr. Applerose, I hope you will join me at supper while these gentlemen are debating your future." They made an impressive exit.

For hospitality on a magnificent saga scale, Alan told himself, you had to hand it to the Norrolanders. A glorious spread had been laid out in the small dining-room, with Hafstalman and two younger Vikings passing dishes and filling glasses. Dobb and Stannsen, Inga and Miss Mick, were already there, and after a few minutes Sir Lancelot turned up from somewhere, a brighter pink than usual, rather goggle-eyed and talking mostly in a high falsetto. There were the usual toasts. Inga and Alan sat very close together. Stannsen described his student days to Miss Mick, who had persuaded him to allow her to write a series of articles about him. Dobb and Dr. Bergenborg argued about world politics. Sir Lancelot tried to fascinate both the younger Vikings. Hafstalman roared with laughter. No reference was made to the meeting of the Star Chamber and to the possible fate of Dobb and Alan, who was very gay but also feeling rather sick.

Then came the pale, eggy Chairman, compromising with one pair of spectacles, and with him was the shortish man with the humorous face. They had brought the verdict. If Dobb and Alan would undertake, first, to abandon any further attempt at broadcasting their own programme, and, secondly, not to make any statements to the press; and if, in addition, Dobb would submit his invention to the authorities; then no proceedings would be taken against them. Alan agreed almost at once, spurred by some hard arm-pinching from Inga. Dobb was hesitant at first, and what decided him was a highly technical question from the shortish man, himself an expert; then Dobb soon agreed, so that he could plunge rapturously into a bewilderingly involved technical discussion with his fellow expert.

"I wish you were half as wrapped up in me as those two are in each other," said Inga, wistfully regarding the technicians.

"I am, my golden poppet," Alan muttered, "but not at a supper table. I need a quiet room, shaded lights, and more ease in the tummy. Don't worry. Now that I'm a free man, I'll be able to pay you so much attention you'll be off your head with ecstatic devotion. Which will be all very well, but might not help you to get the better kind of job, when you have to earn a living for two."

"Oh—darling, I never know whether you're serious or not," she cried. "It's so confusing."

"To be happy, the female must feel confused. You look at the women who live with the non-confusing kinds of men—golfers, stamp collectors, secretaries of photographic societies."

Sir Lancelot rose to his feet rather uncertainly, resting his left hand on the shoulder of the youngest Viking. "Mr. President, ladies and gentlemen," he cried. "I raise my glass to give you a toast."

"Bravo!" This shout came unexpectedly from the eggy-spectacled man, who, liberally assisted by Dr. Bergenborg, must have worked hard to catch up with the rest of them. "What are you going to give us, Telly? Speak up, speak up."

"I would remind our distinguished friend," cried Sir Lancelot, leaning heavily on the youngest Viking and spilling some of the wine he was holding, "that the words of Mercury are harsh after the songs of Apollo—"

"My God—that reminds me," said Miss Mick. "I must phone the paper." She made a kissing sound near Stannsen's shining mahogany dome, and pinched the back of his vast neck. "I'll be back, honeypot."

"The toast I give you, Mr. President, friends, is that great work to which we owe our meeting here to-night and many of the astonishing events we may or may not have witnessed—the work I have been studying night and day—the long-expected and noble work of our friend Stannsen—the Tenth Symphony—"

"Coupled—if you'll forgive the term," Alan shouted, "with the Dobbophone." And they all rose and drank.

The party flowed on. Sir Lancelot, in his highest register, took the youngest Viking on a tour of the American symphony orchestras; Dobb and the humorous expert tried to shout each other down about electronics; Hafstalman and the other young Viking bellowed with laughter; the President filled the glass of the eggy Chairman, now no longer pale, while he tried on more spectacles; Stannsen began singing strange Nordic ditties; Inga began a long account, like the plot of a bad novel, of the private life of her friend, the girl with the lisp and the woodcuts; and Alan, pretending to listen, saw the final subject of his *Suite for Strings* beckoning to him in full *Schnapps-sunlight*.

# CHAPTER IX

# LAST LOW NOTES

ALAN WAS in Radio Centre again, but only as a visitor. He had promised Lancelot to show him Dobb's new recording machine, no larger and heavier than a portable typewriter but astonishingly faithful in its reproduction. So he had it with him. But on the way up to Lancelot's office he had run into Porton, who had insisted upon taking him into his own room. "I was just about to write to you," said Porton, as they went in. "Do you want to nurse that thing. What is it?"

"It's a new musical gadget that Lancelot's interested in," said Alan, fiddling with it in what he hoped looked like an absent-minded fashion. Actually he was switching on the recording device.

"What are you doing now?"

"I've just finished my *Suite for Strings*," said Alan. "Otherwise, nothing. But I'll have to earn some money soon because I hope to get married shortly."

"So I gathered. Now, in spite of the Air Marshal, who was very obstinate at first, I think I've cleared the way for your return here. Once you're back with us — and are working in a co-operative spirit — I see no reason why you shouldn't take over the Directorship of Music from Telly. I'm almost certain I can work it. As I told you some weeks ago, before all the fuss began, some of us aren't happy about Telly. He takes an arrogant, overbearing line at Policy Meetings, as you know. He drinks too much. His private life isn't — well, too reputable. And he obviously neglects the general programme side of his work, anything outside the symphony concerts. Even if the Air Marshal stays — and that's doubtful — I think I can promise that Telly will be out soon. And if you come back to us, then there, my dear Applerose, is your chance. I'd be prepared to back you, so long as certain things were understood between us, and I felt you were co-operating with me on general policy."

"You're definitely at work to get Lancelot out, are you?" said Alan, chiefly for the benefit of the recording apparatus on his knee.

"Not to put too fine a point upon it, you may say I am. The truth is, of course, we need a reshuffle here, and I'm working on it." Porton coughed, then leaned forward and spoke in a lower tone. "I have rather a nice tie-up now with somebody in the Treasury, and at least one good friend in the Lord President's office. This is very much between ourselves, naturally. But there are—shall we say—certain strings that can be pulled—Ah! Come in, Westfort. I'm just having a chat with Applerose."

Westfort, the donnish metaphysical E.B.C. programme planner, shook hands enthusiastically with Alan. "Just the man I wanted to see. In fact, I had a note to write to you—"

"I must say, you chaps seem to have developed a new interest in me," said Alan. "What were you going to write about, Westfort?"

"I'm planning a new game-feature that I'm calling *Postman's Knock*—"

"Any kissing in it?"

"No, after some discussion, we decided against kissing. The sound effect isn't very convincing, and we felt the critics would tell us to transfer the programme from sound radio to TV and we're not ready for that. And of course we have to be very careful these days not to create feelings of frustration in audience response because of a lack of visual imagery. But we're keeping the name *Postman's Knock* because it induces a certain amount of nostalgic reminiscence together with overtones of erotic adolescent feeling, we think. But each member of the team chooses one of a group of strangers, whose identity has been previously explained to the listeners. I'm lining up a strong team. The Warden of Holy Trinity is almost certain. So is the ex-Governor-General of the Baji-Baji Islands—a new strongly masculine type, admirable for our K. to M. groups of listeners, suspected of masochistic tendencies. Then there's Lady Fendether, excellent for identification response from older groups, and little Marigold Dingley, the actress—"

"What groups does she nobble—the sadists?"

"Actually, my dear Applerose, you're not far out. Ask me sometime to show you the report I had on her appeal from Runkler, the psychologist—fascinating. But now we want a fifth member of the team, preferably a man, who could link the feature with the D.

to L. groups—a normal younger type. And I thought about you, Applerose. This Dobb business brought you some useful publicity—why not keep it going with *Postman's Knock*? The fees will soon mount up, for we're repeating the programme on both the North American and Far Eastern services—"

"It must make quite a difference to our standing in the Far East," said Alan, "when they tune in on short wave to hear the Warden of Holy Trinity and little Marigold Thing play *Postman's Knock*. But the answer, Westfort, is *No*."

"Now, give it some thought—"

"It won't bear any thought. I'd rather play games for nitwits than starve, but it hasn't come to that yet. No, Westfort, the man you want is a legal luminary I came across, the other week, called Sir Thomas Something—a powerful personality—dead right for all groups except any I belong to—"

"I'll look him up," said Westfort dubiously. "But let me know if you change your mind. I'll see you later, Porton."

Porton waited a moment or two after the door had closed. "With all due respect to Westfort," he began, "I'm afraid he's slipping. A good mind, undoubtedly, but is it an E.B.C. mind? Some of us think not. But this Telly business is more important. I repeat, this is your chance. What do you say?"

"No, thank you," said Alan promptly. "I wouldn't do at all. No improvement on Lancelot. I'd take an equally arrogant line at Policy Meetings. I drink too much too. My private life isn't very disreputable yet—but give it time. Finally, I'd be even worse than he is about the general programme side of the job, murdering the Twilight Players and the rest of 'em. Sorry, Porton. The truth is, I'm like you—"

"Indeed, Applerose!" Porton sounded surprised. "In what way?"

"I hate radio and the E.B.C. Well, I must now find Lancelot."

"You won't, of course—"

"Tell him?" Alan, lovingly gripping the recording machine, turned at the door to grin at the anxious Porton. "Not one syllable shall pass these lips, Porton. With all due respect—good-day."

He had a little chat first with Mrs. Crisp in the outer office. Mrs. Crisp was very happy. A melancholy Irish drunk, who had been rashly taken on by the Fourth Programme and then kicked out after he had almost wrecked three features, was now well under her wing, where he was sharing her board and bed. "He's so sweet, Alan," she cried, "except sometimes when he's sober. He can talk for hours about the Sidhe—you know, the Irish fairy folk. He says I'm like one of them he once saw. Poor darling Padraic! Why don't you and Miss Dobb come to dinner. You'd both adore him."

"As soon as things are rather easier, we will. Dear Mrs. Crisp!" He regarded her fondly. "Don't let him bring any leprechauns into the flat—they're so hard to get out afterwards. Now please tell Lancelot I'm here. By the way, you're not finding any young Vikings round here these days, are you? You're not? I'm delighted to hear it."

Sir Lancelot was wearing a ginger-coloured tweed jacket and a green and yellow striped waistcoat with red glass buttons. His high collar and black satin tie were vaguely Regency. "I like it," said Alan. "A sort of compromise between Beau Brummell, Mr. Jorrocks and Sam Weller. One of your best so far, Lancelot. Now this is Dobb's recording machine. You see—small, compact, comparatively light— and superbly faithful. Let you hear it in a minute. You haven't a cigar, by any chance?"

"You can have a dozen, Alan, my boy." Sir Lancelot threw a small and very fancy box. "That Mexican composer presented me with 'em. Probably too strong even for you."

"Not at all. A man needs a good strong cigar here in Radio Centre. Porton's been trying to persuade me to rejoin you."

"Well, why don't you? I told the Air Marshal last week we needed you. Come, my dear Alan, they really aren't so bad, you know. Even these fellows like Porton. We have our differences, of course." Sir Lancelot waved them away, which helped to rid him of some of the Mexican fumes that were now coming his way. "But in spite of everything, there's a sort of *camaraderie*—a certain loyalty you discover after a time—"

"Hold it, Lancelot. I want you to listen to this recording. The quality below the usual level, because, for a reason that'll soon be obvious, I didn't pull the mike out. But it'll do, I fancy. Now listen, *camarade.*" He was now ready to switch on, and did.

Sir Lancelot listened with mild amusement until he heard Porton say, "I see no reason why you shouldn't take over the Directorship of Music from Telly. I'm almost certain I can work it." After that his pink gradually changed to a horrible purple, his eyes bulged, his breathing quickened; he was like a bomb with a spluttering fuse. "That's enough," he yelled finally. "Turn it off. Never mind about Westfort and his idiotic parlour games—"

"But wouldn't you like to hear me telling Porton I'd be even worse than you?"

"No. I know what you'd say. But—my God—either that creeping little red-tape worm clears out of this building—or I do. I'll present Block with an ultimatum. Arrogant? Porton doesn't know what arrogance is yet—but I'll show him. And that filthy stuff about my private life. He hasn't any private life. When he leaves here, he turns into nothing. He doesn't eat, doesn't drink, has no friends, and has about as much sex life as a Government White Paper. He's—he's a talking insect." Sir Lancelot was striding up and down the room now. He stopped for a moment, however, glaring wildly in Alan's direction, as if words were failing him.

"You were saying, Lancelot," said Alan smoothly, "that in spite of differences here, there's a certain loyalty—a sort of *camaraderie*—"

"Stop it, you young devil. Though it serves me right for talking such dam' bosh. I only wanted to get you back because you've always been so useful to me. But of course you're quite right. Stay out. If it wasn't for those hellish railway hotels, I'd walk straight out now—"

"What railway hotels?" Alan was genuinely puzzled.

Sir Lancelot suddenly looked quite old. "My dear boy, an orchestral conductor in this country must accept provincial engagements. And provincial engagements mean railway hotels. Those appalling cold suppers—the fatty ham soaked with beetroot juice, the lump of lettuce, the two tomatoes, the soggy trifle, the mouse-trap cheese— the yawning night porter who can only find you bottled beer—the commercial travellers talking about football—the icy hell of the bedroom. Imagine all that after you've just finished conducting the Brahms Number One, sweating like a maniac, with pneumonia lurking in those draughty rooms behind the platform. Imagine having six *Messiahs* to conduct, in places like Hull and Burnley, with the country fog-bound. My boy, I sometimes think I'm paying in this life, here in this joyless country, for all my splendid scarlet sins in previous existences, which unfortunately I can't even remember. I talk about walking out of this place—but what'll happen if I do? Don't tell me, I know. Ninety minutes of Tschaikowsky in Wolverhampton. Sleet, a heavy cold, and the Mendelssohn Violin Concerto in Birkenhead—"

Mildred Povey came in, bringing with her a very tall young man with one of the longest necks and smallest heads Alan had ever seen.

She had the air of having brought him alive out of Central Africa. "Sir Lancelot, Mrs. Crisp said it was only Alan who was here, so I knew you wouldn't mind—"

In point of fact, Miss Povey," said Sir Lancelot, who hated to be interrupted like this, "I do mind." He looked at the giraffe type. "How d'you do? I don't think we've met, have we?"

"As a metter of fect, we haven't," said the very tall young man, "though ectually I'm often here—"

"Sir Lancelot, this is Reg Tabb, the poet," cried Mildred. "Alan Applerose—Reg. We're engaged."

"We're not," said Alan very quickly, starting up in alarm.

"Don't be a fool, Alan. I mean—Reg and I are engaged. How's the little Dobb girl? I hope you'll be happy. I think she's probably the type you need. I've just started rehearsing a marvellous verse play by Reg for the Fourth."

"Ectually," said Reg, with a serpentine motion of the neck, "it's called *Edna Wants to Sell Vesuvius*. The idea—"

"Just a moment," cried Sir Lancelot. He began laughing. "It's silly—but I really thought for a second that you said *Edna Wants to Sell Vesuvius*. It just shows—"

"As a metter of fect," said Reg coldly, "I did say *Edna Wants to Sell Vesuvius*—"

Sir Lancelot stopped him, then turned to Alan. "Y'know, Alan, it still sounds to me—"

"Like Edna selling Vesuvius," said Alan. "Well, that's what she is doing—or wants to do. I'll bet it's whimsical, very lyrical in places but with some bitter thrusts at suburbia. Isn't it, Reg?"

"Shut up, Alan." This was Mildred.

"It's wit and phentasy," said Reg. "The kind of thing Mildred does so well. And Derek is going to be febulous in it—ebsolutely febulous. He plays Edna's grendfather though ectually in my play he's younger than she is."

"I like that, Reg," said Alan. "By the way, Westfort's looking for a fifth member of a team to play Postman's Knock. If you could guarantee reasonable identity response from, say, groups B. to K., I believe you'd be dead right—"

"For God's sake!" Sir Lancelot almost screamed. Then he closed his eyes. "Sometimes I think I must be going out of my mind." He opened his eyes, to stare accusingly at Mildred. "What do you want,

Miss Povey?"

"Oh—yes. It's about the Stannsen concert. I wondered—"

"Tickets? Not a hope, my dear girl. I can't do a thing for you."

"Well—really—I must say—"

"I've had to say No to some of my oldest and dearest friends," said Sir Lancelot. "Not a chance, I assure you. Just put it out of your head."

"Thank you," cried Mildred bitterly. "Come along, Reg." And she swept him out.

"By the way, Lancelot," said Alan, "Inga and I dined with Stannsen last night, and then I went through his own copy of the score with him. There are one or two points—"

"My dear boy, this is just what I want. Let's lunch—I can deal with Porton later—and talk it over. I'm worried about the Second Movement—and of course the Finale—I haven't rehearsed that damned Dobbophone yet. Dobb's coming to-morrow—and I hope you will too. And you must bring Stannsen with you to the final run-through—that's essential. I'm depending on you for that, my dear boy."

Although this final rehearsal was in the morning before the concert, it was decided to use the big studio at Radio Centre; the Festival Hall itself would be noisy with engineers and workmen preparing it for the evening's great occasion. Inga went along with Alan and Stannsen. Dobb was already there, sitting high in the orchestra behind his shiny black monster. As soon as Sir Lancelot saw Stannsen, he called the orchestra to attention, and the men jumped up and began clapping or tapping on their fiddles with the backs of their bows. Stannsen replied with a wide grin and a wave of the hand. "No thanks you," he replied to Sir Lancelot. "No speech. I never make speeches. You make speech. I think you make nice speech."

Sir Lancelot, who was wearing some sort of Russian blouse and black velveteen pants, climbed on to the improvised rostrum, motioned the players into their seats, and proceeded to enjoy himself in his grandest manner. "I need hardly tell you that you are about to play in the presence of the most distinguished living composer." There was more applause, to which Stannsen, now seated between Inga and Alan, listened with a sardonic detachment. "You and I," Sir Lancelot continued, in his most impressive style, "are about to attempt an interpretation of this master's latest and perhaps greatest work—the Tenth Symphony—of which we shall be giving to-night the first performance. This is, as you all realize, a very great honour indeed, a proud privilege for which we offer the composer our most grateful thanks. During the thirty years I have been conducting symphonic music, no greater honour or privilege than this has come my way. I can say, with truth, with deepest sincerity, with warmest gratitude, that I count this my proudest hour." He made an immense sweeping gesture, stepped back, and fell off the rostrum.

Quarter of an hour later, his moans subsiding under morphia, he was removed to a hospital, the doctor explaining that even apart from the broken leg, Sir Lancelot was in poor shape, and might with luck be able to conduct again in about three or four months' time. The big studio sounded like Bedlam.

"All is simple," Stannsen roared at Alan above the din. "You conduct to-night. Why not? Now you know the work. And you are better musician. I am happy for you. All is simple."

"All isn't simple," said Alan. "I haven't even a clean dress shirt. Or a decent white waistcoat—"

"Don't be silly, darling," cried Inga. "What sizes do you take? I'll go and get everything you want. Now tell me. I think it's wonderful."

While he was hastily giving her instructions, Air Marshal Block arrived, the strong man in a crisis. One of his dithering entourage introduced him to Stannsen. "Nuisance, this, Dr. Stannsen," he said bluffly. "Can't cancel to-night, y'know. Everybody's coming—everything fixed up—can't possibly cancel. We'll find you a decent conductor somehow, though. Beecham, Boult, Sargent—one of those fellas, if he's free. Don't worry."

"I don't worry," said Stannsen. "Here is conductor." He pointed to Alan. "He knows work now. Good musician. I am happy for him."

"I dare say you are." The Air Marshal made a barking sound that was meant to suggest laughter. "But are we? That's the point. I don't think so. Can't have Applerose, I'm afraid. Various good reasons. Doesn't carry the guns, anyhow."

"Guns? We do not want guns. We want good musician."

"Well, we'll find you a reliable fella. See you through. Don't worry." And he was about to turn away.

Stannsen exploded into Norrolandish, probably dreadful oaths from remote and bloody sagas.

"I don't get you," said the Air Marshal, frowning. "By the way, I'm

Air Marshal Block—in charge here."

"And I am Stannsen—Stannsen—Stannsen. And I say this younger Applerose take my work to-night."

"Sorry, can't agree. Question of policy."

Stannsen roared like a wounded bull. The executive E.B.C. types who had been clustering round now stepped back, looking alarmed. "You go fly airplanes," he roared. "This is music—music—music. And I say—no Applerose, then no Stannsen symphony, no concert, no nothing. I care not. I get fifty orchestras—hundred orchestras—play my work. I say go to hell. Where is leader of orchestra?" he bellowed. "Come here, leader of orchestra." People made way for Jarritt, the leader, one of Alan's friends, with whom he had often played chamber music. "I ask you, leader," said Stannsen, "is Applerose good conductor for your orchestra?"

"If he knows the work," Jarritt began, giving Alan an enquiring glance.

"I know the work, Jarritt," said Alan quietly.

"Then we'll be very happy with him, Dr. Stannsen. He's handled us often enough."

"A very important occasion to-night, remember," the Air Marshal growled. "A junior fella conducting—fella mixed up in this Dobb business too—it won't look well—"

"Look well—look well? I wish it to sound well," roared Stannsen. "You bring new conductor now to read my score—it will sound damned stinking awful—"

"He's probably right," said Jarritt to the Air Marshal. "It's not an easy work."

"And I have explain what I want to Applerose, who is my friend," said Stannsen. Then he showed signs of exploding again. "I say no more. In one minute I go—"

"Very well," said the Air Marshal. "Get cracking, Applerose. And don't let us down."

"I'll try not to let the music down," said Alan. "Right, Jarritt. Give the boys a shout. No, Mamber, I've no time for publicity stories. We've a lot of work to do here."

They had three hours of it. Alan enjoyed every minute of them. He had never thought of himself as a conductor, he had no reputation to lose. He had gone through the score more than once with Stannsen himself, had discussed it with Lancelot. Even so, if he had had a week's notice that he was to conduct this concert, he might have developed nerves; but now there was no time for his self-confidence to dwindle. And it was fun bringing in Dobb and his monster, which could just be heard for a few bars, in a *fortissimo* passage, a mile below the passionate strings, the triumphant woodwind, horns and trumpets, like some dinosaur in the bottom of the Grand Canyon. Alan could not be quite sure Dobb was always playing the right notes, if they could be called notes, and certainly his time was faulty at first and had to be corrected. Twice, Dobb lost his temper, probably because he could see and hear Stannsen below, roaring with laughter. But the two of them went off together, still growling at each other, at the end of the rehearsal, while Inga, with her purchases, went home with Alan to make sure he would be nicely dressed. She left him in good time, to make sure that she was even more nicely dressed; and Alan went through the evening's scores again. Even now he was not exactly nervous; but nothing except the music itself seemed quite real. It was rather like the hollow, featureless time just before an operation.

Probably there were a few hundred people in the packed Festival Hall who cared about music; but no more. All the other seats were filled with highest-level personages, assorted V.I.P.s and those people who must by hook or crook be present at occasions of this kind, the starers-at-royalty, the recognizers of famous faces, the "We were there that night" couples, the people who are always paying five guineas a seat to see and hear something they cannot enjoy but are happy sharing a roof, however large, with the great. They make a dead audience, as Alan soon realized. He decided to dislike them, if only to keep up his self-confidence. The first part of the concert consisted of an early tone poem of Stannsen's and the Third Symphony, probably his best-known work. The orchestra could have played them adequately without Alan, and in certain passages they almost did, especially in the long slow movement of the Third, which was Stannsen at his weakest and had bored Alan for years. But just to show there was no ill-feeling, except towards most of the audience, sitting there wondering what to have for supper, he really took charge of the boys in the last ten minutes, lashed them along in a frenzy, and achieved a dazzling finale. He took four recalls and made the orchestra stand up. His final gestures were so deeply modest and self-effacing that he felt he must look as if he were trying to sell the people in the front row a few Oriental rugs.

While he was changing his collar in the conductor's room, Dobb, who had yet to make his appearance on the platform, looked in. He was wearing greenish tails of a strange old-fashioned cut; his hair stood on end; his red-leathery face was almost purple; he was smoking a cigar and was carrying a large flask, which contained something he had obviously had several of already.

"Hello—that cigar's tantalizing," said Alan. "Meant to bring one—but forgot."

"Got it here for you, m'boy." And there it was, a beauty. "Better have a nip or two as well, hadn't you?" He pushed the flask under Alan's nose.

"Just one perhaps." He had a drink and Dobb followed him with suspicious haste. "By the way, you're not pickled, are you?"

"Certainly not." Dobb was indignant. "Just hungry, that's all. Daren't eat. Man can't play the Dobbophone and eat. I won't say I haven't had a few drinks. Can't help it. Been practising. And a man can't play the Dobbophone and not drink. Must drink—take it out of you. Matter of fact—take another nip, Alan, you'll need it—she's not as young as she was and I've used her pretty damned hard lately, especially to-day—"

"Who's this?"

"Dobbophone, of course, m'boy." Dobb tackled the flask again, still staring at Alan sombrely. Then he lowered both the flask and his voice. "Between you and me, Alan, she's rather temperamental to-night. My fault, of course. I always meant to improve that valve—but thought it might see me through—"

"My hat! You don't mean to say—"

"No, no, no, no. It ought to see us through. Tricky, though. Her first real public appearance too. Well, that's life—"

"Never mind about life," said Alan, now thoroughly alarmed. "You put that flask away and hurry back to your Dobbophone. Look—we haven't much time—"

"Thought Stannsen might be coming round. Good thing he's not, perhaps."

"He's being presented and all that—somewhere out there. They wanted me to go but I begged off—said I'd have to change. Now listen, Dobb—one last word. I'll bring you in exactly as I did this morning—"

"Don't worry, Alan. Remember everything—all under control. It's just a question now whether she behaves herself. Best of luck." He shook hands with a solemnity that Alan did not at all like the look of, and departed in a slow majestic manner that was not reassuring.

Alan was waiting to go on the platform when Dobb, rather late, very slowly climbed into his high place, carrying the fabulous instrument. There had not been all that publicity about it for nothing. Cheers followed murmurs of recognition and ripples of laughter, and then there was a solid round of applause, which Dobb, whom Alan could just see from the side, gravely acknowledged.

"He couldn't have had a few, could he?" said Jarritt, who was waiting to make his late entrance, as leader.

"He could—and has," Alan groaned.

"If he lets that thing fall forward, it'll mow down half the woodwind—"

"Stop, for God's sake. There's an invisible malice department just waiting to pick up ideas like that. Get on, Jarritt, and smirk at 'em. Let's get this over with."

But the dark, handsome young conductor who made his bow, a minute or two later, looked perfectly at ease; and about a hundred and fifty women, almost up to the highest level, made a mental note to put him on their dining lists. And now Stannsen's great Tenth Symphony became part of men's heritage; it was full of wisdom, mockery and tenderness, lit with that clear flame which burns in some elderly geniuses, those who create out of the fullness and not the frustrated poverty of experience. Alan forgot everything—all the high-level nonsense, the worldwide hook-ups, the critics, the E.B.C.—except the music and the fact that Stannsen himself, who had chosen him, was listening. This was Stannsen's creation, and Alan tried to interpret it in the light of his knowledge of the man, his admiration and affection for him. The orchestra was no longer ninety grumbling instrumentalists, wondering about their teeth and taxes, they were spirits newly released from the wrong planet; Alan led them to within sight of the fields of Paradise. Even during the last movement, when he had to fling the stick towards Dobb to bring him in, Alan lived with the music, forgetting all the arguments and publicity and nonsense, sketching with his flickering baton and eloquent left hand the noble architecture of the movement, moving through despair and hope to the great resolving final chords. He soared and sang and thundered with the boys. God in Heaven—but they were home. Crash! Hold it, boys. Crash! Hold it, hold it. Now then—doomsday—*cr-a-a-a-ash*!

At the fifth recall, while they were bringing Stannsen round to the platform, Alan, now ready for any devilment, pointed at Dobb and his monster. The players, grinning, turned to applaud, and the audience clapped and cheered, so that Dobb, purple and furious, had to bow. Then Stannsen arrived, massive and smiling, and before he acknowledged the existence of the audience, now noisier than ever, he shook hands with Alan and made a vast gesture of thanks to the orchestra, as if embracing them all. Then he too singled out Dobb, and began roaring with laughter. By the time he was off the platform, Alan was roaring with laughter too; and five minutes later, back in Alan's room, Dobb, after a first explosion, was roaring with them.

That is how Inga, after much difficulty, found them—two old idiots and one young one, not telling one another what a wonderful night it had been, not living up to the occasion at all, but drinking, wheezing, spluttering, slapping each other on the back, and laughing like lunatics. She was annoyed. She had been deeply moved by the music and by the sight of Alan there, so much admired by everybody, had wanted to tell him at once what she felt—and now, with the infuriating perversity of the male, especially this kind of male, they were behaving like idiots.

"Oh—do stop it!" she cried. She had locked the door behind her, for the corridor was filling with people. "And there are masses of people wanting to see you—"

"Well, they can't see us," said Alan, wiping his eyes. "Have a drink, darling?"

"No, not just now. And I think you three ought to wait. You look awful and you sound awful—"

"We *are* awful," said her uncle, still wheezing and spluttering.

Stannsen, busy with the bottle, burst into yet another roar of laughter.

"Oh—you are stupid. I could shake you."

By a tremendous effort, Stannsen controlled himself. He wagged a finger at the indignant Inga. "How you think Uncle Roland played? Good, you think? Many people think so, eh? Dobbophone is success?"

"It was all absolutely wonderful—even the Dobbophone. Everybody's saying so. Now stop being silly, you three."

But they laughed and laughed again, spilling drink down their shirt-fronts. "I'm going if you don't stop. What on earth is it, anyhow? Just some men's idiocy—babyish nonsense—"

"We must tell her," said Alan.

Stannsen looked at her. "Can you keep great secret?"

"Yes, if I really have to, what is it?"

Stannsen took another drink, smacking his lips over it. "Has been big trouble over Dobbophone, you know, Inga—"

"I should think I do. Haven't I been up to the neck in it from the start. Well?"

"This is secret. You promise to keep? Good!" Stannsen looked at her; his eyes began to water; he exploded again. Dobb joined him. But this time Alan behaved sensibly. He put his arms round her, gave her a kiss, and said, "You look beautiful, my golden bunny. I love you. They love you too. But, you see—and this is the secret—not a single note ever came out of that Dobbophone to-night. It just wouldn't play."

There was some determined knocking on the door, voices outside. Inga unlocked the door and opened it a few inches. The most urgent demands were from press photographers, who had found the Dobbophone but not Dobb. Inga pushed him out to satisfy them, but at the request of Alan, who said he would have to change in a minute or two, she locked the door again. As they began talking, he removed his collar, tie, coat and waistcoat, and then went into the little dressing-room to remove the rest.

"You know, Alan, I have idea," said Stannsen. "This is for you too, Inga, if you wish to marry."

"Of course I wish to marry," cried Inga. "But Alan says he'll have to sell his grand piano, and I don't want him to have to do that."

"No selling piano," Stannsen shouted. "No selling any things. I have idea. Alan, you are for me fine conductor."

"Very nice of you to say so," Alan called from the dressing-room. "I did better to-night than I thought I would. Got 'em through all right. But of course I'm not the real top thing."

"You talk foolish," cried Stannsen angrily. "I do not like real top thing, you call him. I tell you, I am tired of these conductors who have big temperament, big personality, much show-off. I will not listen to them play my music. It is their music, not my music. I want my music. To-night you give me my music as written. It is Stannsen Tenth Symphony—not film star Luna Park Tenth Symphony for showing off conductor. So now I say this. You want to play my Tenth Symphony—very good—you have Alan Applerose conduct—no other. Anywhere—any orchestra—it must be the same. For two years only Alan Applerose conduct my Tenth Symphony."

Alan popped a dripping head out of the dressing-room, to stare at Stannsen. "You really mean that? You're not just trying to help us—"

"I like to help, yes," Stannsen shouted. "If little Inga want money, I give her money. But this is some things different. This is music. So I do it to help myself—not you. I know you play this work as I want it to be played. So I have not to travel, to rehearse, to be angry with big film star conductors—it is fine for me. It is fine for you too, I think."

"It's wonderful," cried Inga, embracing him. "It's perfect. I'll go everywhere too, and I adore travelling. But will Uncle Roland have to come too?"

"No—no—Dobbophone finished. It was all foolishness. I think I double *contra-bass bassoon*. What you say, Alan?"

"I think so," the invisible Alan called out. Then they heard him laughing. "I've suddenly remembered I never told you about those other three mad instruments, including the two-man quadruple bass fiddle from Clermont-Ferrand. Twins, they were. I wonder what's become of them?"

Three nights later he knew. He and Inga were sitting in a box at the North London Hippodrome with the Fettles, who were celebrating the twentieth anniversary of their marriage. "I hear it's a good all-round show this week," Joe had said after dinner, when he and Alan lit two majestic Havanas, "and there's one little surprise in it for you. So don't ask me to buy any programmes—an' don't buy one yourself."

"Now don't overdo it, Joe," his wife had said. "It won't be much of a surprise. I'm sure I don't care about it, and I don't believe they will. Still, they say it is a good show this week. And, anyhow, you'll be together, you two, holding hands and all that. I must show you what Joe's bought me."

So there they were, rather sleepy but well content, in the box at the Hippodrome, at the second house. Joe's surprise came just after the interval, for the elegant couple who sang a little into the mike, exchanged a few mild jokes, and then did some ballroom dancing, were none other than Kenneth and Daphne Perman. "She made it, see?" said Joe complacently. "Publicity she got from Dobb's radio did the trick at last. They're in."

"But how far?" said Inga. "He's not very good but he's better than she is."

"Just what I was thinking, dear," said Mrs. Fettle. "She'll never be anything, if you ask me. Not at *this*, anyhow. Well, I told you it wasn't much of a surprise."

"This next is a new act that's goin' over big, they tell me," said Joe. "Manager here's an old pal of mine, an' he says this next act's booked for the Palladium—an' it isn't even American."

The band played some odd music, made up of squeals and growls. The red velvet parted and lifted to reveal a large insane drawing-room with everything in it queerly shaped and not standing up straight. Alan took to it at once. "This is my stuff, whatever it is," he told Inga. And then he let out a shout of joy. For there they were, in baggy evening clothes, with white faces and vast painted grins, staggering beneath their monstrous instruments—Herr Julius Grobemeier, of Mannheim, and Signor Nicola Bertini, of Milan. This was glorious, but not yet reaching ecstasy, for where were Alfred and Louis Sauvager, of Clermont-Ferrand? If they were not in the act, then Inga and the Fettles would never believe they really existed, could never be made to share his vision of those identical twins, with their wasted, glaring look and unreal blue-black moustaches, and their unbelievable two-man fiddle. Alas—alas! But no, something was about to happen, somebody was making a big entrance. Yes, they were here. They marched on carrying the giant fiddle on their shoulders; they wore very skimpy evening suits with severe high collars; they were indistinguishable, not a hair different; their moustaches were if anything a bluer-black; they glared fanatically at the conductor. Speaking together in rapid and passionate French, as fanatical as their eyes, they prepared to perform, waving aside the two lumbering and bewildered clowns, the monster brass and woodwind. Still talking at full speed, one of them climbed on to the little platform to manipulate the strings, the other grasped the giant bow with both hands. They stopped talking. They bowed, severely. A terrible blast from the *Great-German-Double-Bombardon* filled them with resentment. A challenge from the black and shining monster of Milan enraged them. They hissed together like maddened serpents. They glared at the conductor again. They were off, plucking and sawing like maniacs; Mannheim and Milan were joining them; the

North London Hippodrome was in danger of coming apart; and Alan could not see properly, was almost lost in a red haze, in the ache and glory of his laughter.

"What's so incredible and wonderful," he announced later, sweating over drinks and sandwiches in the tropics of the Fettle sitting-room, "is that everybody's got something. The Permans. Not much, but it's what they wanted. Those fabulous foreigners, who'll probably tour the world now, for they'll be equally idiotic and glorious in any country. Stannsen's had his joke with Dobb and successfully launched his symphony, and of course—ahem—found the perfect conductor. Dobb himself is happily dickering with the Government over his radio gadgets. Even poor old Sir Lancelot, whom I saw this morning, by the way, is having a rest he needs and beginning to enjoy himself. Mildred Povey has her Reg, who ectually as a metter of fect will suit her perfectly. Dr. Bergenborg—bless him—has his trade agreement, with much kudos and schnapps-all-round in Norroland. Even that tough wench, Helen Mick, Stannsen says, has sold her Stannsen articles to America—and in addition, I fancy, has—"

"Yes, we know," said Inga. "Wicked old man! But what have I got?"

"You? Why, me, of course."

"That's right, dear," cried Mrs. Fettle. "And very lucky you are, both of you. Like Joe and me."

"To say nothing," Alan continued, waving half a sandwich at Inga, "of those five high-class pieces of airplane luggage that we've bought and can't afford. Probably if we knew about Air Marshal Block and Dr. Trock—he's the Betrothal Breaking expert at the Norroland Embassy, Joe—we'd find they'd got something very cosy. As for me—by crikey—I've got everything—Inga, Stannsen's Tenth Symphony, the sack from the E.B.C., the entry into *Schnapps-sunlight*—"

"Not if I can help it," Inga told him.

"And enough rich experience, glowing in the memory, to keep me reminiscing at the stove-side through the longest Norroland night. I tell you, Miss Dobb, Mr. and Mrs. Fettle, we have here a glimpse, just a glimpse, of the working of the Great Plan. It was first revealed to me by an airman, a splendid heroic fellow but full of sensibility too, with whom I once shared a railway dining-table, between Salisbury and Waterloo, and one of the worst meals I ever remember. He asked me what I thought was the most significant sentence in all English literature, and then gave me his choice. It's the statement by the Dodo at the end of the caucus-race in *Alice In Wonderland* when the others ask it who has won. Do you remember? The Dodo said, *'Everybody has won, and all must have prizes.'* Well, that's us."

"Darling," cried Inga.

Also available from Great Northern Books:

# Sir Michael and Sir George:
*A Tale of COMSA and DISCUS and the New Elizabethans*
**by J.B. Priestley**

*'Most people here don't give a damn about scholarship and the arts, and they include nearly all the men who are running the country. They may pretend to, but they don't really care ...'*

Deadly rivals Sir Michael Stratherrick (womaniser and Director of COMSA) and Sir George Drake (Director of DISCUS with little interest in the arts) are threatened with extinction. Her Majesty's Treasury plans to abolish both organisations and set up a new and expanded arts department within the Ministry of Higher Education. There can only be room for one director. So begins a contemptuous fight for survival with both men and their organisations seeking to out-manoeuvre and undermine each other at every turn. As the action moves through the shire counties and the North of England, the strip-tease bars of Soho and the plush surroundings of expense account Mayfair, things become even more complicated as we learn that along with their jobs, Sir George's marriage and Sir Michael's carefree single days are also under threat.

With Priestley's characteristic humanity and sympathy for his characters' plights, this tremendously entertaining satire attacks the whole world of subsidised arts councils, those who support them with public money, civil service bureaucrats and the machinations of Government politics.

As bureaucracy and the reach of Government continue to expand, this is very much a relevant novel for our time.

*'To me Priestley was a writer who produced work of dazzling variety and rich profusion. He was wise and had integrity.'*
**Stan Barstow**

*'As a writer of fiction he belongs in a great English realist tradition that includes Bennett, Wells and Galsworthy.'*
**Michael Billington**

J. B. Priestley titles from Great Northern Books:

*Novels*

**Angel Pavement**
**Bright Day**
**Lost Empires**
**The Good Companions**
**Low Notes on a High Level**
**Sir Michael and Sir George**

*Non-fiction*

**English Journey**
**Delight**

*Biography*

**Priestley at Kissing Tree House: A Memoir**
by Rosalie Batten
J. B. Priestley's Personal Secretary 1968-1984

**Britain Speaks**
*J.B. Priestley broadcasts to the World*
by Austin Mitchell

www.greatnorthernbooks.co.uk